THE ROAD TO CANTERBURY

The Road to Canterbury

TALES FROM CHAUCER
RETOLD BY
IAN SERRAILLIER

ILLUSTRATED WITH WOOD ENGRAVINGS BY
JOHN LAWRENCE

HEINEMANN
NEW WINDMILLS

Heinemann Educational Books Ltd
Halley Court, Jordan Hill, Oxford OX2 8EJ
OXFORD   LONDON   EDINBURGH
MADRID   ATHENS   BOLOGNA   PARIS
MELBOURNE   SYDNEY   AUCKLAND
IBADAN   NAIROBI   HARARE   GABORONE
SINGAPORE   TOKYO   PORTSMOUTH NH (USA)

ISBN 0 435 12259 2

95 96 97 98 99 13 12 11 10 9

To Jane

Printed in England by Clays Ltd, St Ives plc

CONTENTS

6 *Contents*

INTRODUCING
GEOFFREY CHAUCER

GEOFFREY CHAUCER (1340?–1400) was the earliest great poet and story-teller in English literature. He was born in London, in Thames Street, by the busy waterway and port, not far from the Tower of London. His father was a prosperous wine-merchant, whose family had been in the wine trade for several generations. Close to his home were the docks where French, Spanish and Italian wines were unloaded. There were anchorages for sea-going boats, and wharves from which English wool and cloth were shipped abroad.

Here, in the cosmopolitan society of trade, with plenty to store away in his mind and stimulate his imagination, the boy was brought up. He would have been taught to read before he went to school – perhaps by a clerk in lower orders anxious to add to his slender income. There were three grammar schools in London, and he was probably sent to the one nearest his home, St Paul's Almonry. Latin was the principal subject taught. French he would have picked up at home and among the wine-merchants, as well as what he learnt at school. The upper and middle classes all spoke French. Religion, reading, arithmetic, and possibly some natural science were also school subjects.

In 1357 he went off to be page in the household of the Countess of Ulster, a daughter-in-law of King Edward III. His duties included making beds, holding and carrying torches, and taking messages for the chamberlain. At night he slept on the floor of the great hall. He met courtiers and statesmen, soldiers and ambassadors, artists, musicians, craftsmen. When some time later he was promoted to squire, he was allowed to share a small room and a servant with a fellow squire, and his wages rose to 7½d a day. We do not know when he started writing poems, but his *The Book of the Duchess* (1369) reflects the experiences of this period. No doubt he was writing experimentally. Penning verses to a lady love, as well as drawing and composing music, were common accomplishments for a squire. The squire in the Prologue to *The Canterbury Tales* is no exception:

> Poet he was, composer, and, what's more,
> Could dance, joust in the lists and write and draw.

In 1359 Chaucer was sent abroad to fight the French in what is now called the Hundred Years War. He was still a squire (roughly the same as a second lieutenant in the modern army) and never rose to the higher rank of knight. That winter he was taken prisoner near Rheims. The following year he was ransomed for £16 (perhaps £3,000 in modern money) and went home. He probably lacked the temperament for soldiering, but there were other ways in which he could be useful to the Crown. King Edward III must have thought highly of him, for he paid part of the ransom himself.

In 1366 or thereabouts Chaucer married Philippa de Roet, lady-in-waiting to the Queen and sister of John of Gaunt's third wife. John of Gaunt was a son of King Edward III. Love played little part in a medieval marriage, and it is doubtful if in this union Chaucer found any true companionship. Marriages were usually arranged by parents or friends. His allusions to married life are mostly ironical and seldom flattering. Although at that time a wife was expected to defer to her husband and obey him, the nagging and boisterous Wife of Bath in *The Canterbury Tales* could hardly be said to follow this pattern.

In 1373 he was sent to Italy for the first time – he was to return again in 1378 – on the King's business, probably a trade mission. The visit brought him into contact with the finest art and literature in the world. The Gothic architecture of Pisa, Florence and Genoa was fresh and new. Giotto, the painter and sculptor, had died only recently, and the arts were flourishing. The poet Dante, to whose style he owes so much, had died in 1321. But Petrarch and Boccaccio, the greatest writers of the day, from whose poems and stories Chaucer borrowed so freely, were still alive, and he may even have met them.

On his return to London in 1374 he was made Controller of Customs on wools, skins and hides in the Port of London, a post he held till 1386. He continued to travel abroad on the King's business. From the King he received a pitcher of wine daily for life, and from John of Gaunt a life-pension. The Corporation of the City of London gave him the house over the Aldgate in the city wall, where he remained till at least 1385. From the west windows he could look out on the crowded narrow street, on roof tops and a hundred church spires. From the east he could see hills and un-hedged fields. In those days the countryside, which he always loved, came right up to the city walls. Here is a modern version of some lines he wrote about his favourite wild flower:

> Of all the flowers of the field, I've said
> That most I love the daisy white and red.
> When winter's gone and comes the month of May,
> I'm out of bed at break of every day
> To wander through the fields, now night is done,
> And see the daisy open in the sun.
> (That's why people call it – well they may –
> The 'day's eye' or else the 'eye of day'.)
> I love it, for it lifts the saddest hours,
> So fresh, so fair, the flower of all flowers.
> At last, when evening comes, swiftly I run
> To see the petals close at set of sun;
> It hates the darkness and it fears the night,
> And on and on it sleeps till morning light.

The passage comes from *The Legend of Good Women* (1384–6). The ten-syllable 'heroic couplet' – here used in English for the first time – became the principal verse form of *The Canterbury Tales* and remained popular with English poets for many centuries to come.

These years were probably the happiest time of Chaucer's life. His job was not too demanding, and he had more time for study than he had ever had at court. He wrote, in the fashionable French style, *The Parliament of Birds* (c. 1377–82), a St Valentine's Day poem, with birds chattering together in sprightly and dramatic conversations. In the Italian style he wrote *Troilus and Criseyde* (c. 1372–84), a romantic poem in five books, sometimes called the first novel in English. Poet, diplomat and man of business, Chaucer was now a person of wealth and position. In 1386 he was made a Justice of the Peace for Kent and a Knight of the Shire, a position similar to that of an M.P.

The same year his good fortune changed. His patron, John of Gaunt, was sent on a military expedition to Spain, and Chaucer lost all his offices. Perhaps the blow to him may now be regarded as a blessing for us, as it gave him the leisure to start on the greatest of his poems, *The Canterbury Tales.*

Even so, his public career was not yet over. In 1389 John of Gaunt returned to favour, and the young King Richard II appointed Chaucer Clerk of the Works. He saw to the maintenance of the Palace of Westminster, the Tower of London, St George's Chapel at Windsor, Berkhamstead Castle, and a number of royal residences, as well as of all the walls, ditches, drains and bridges between Greenwich and Woolwich. Perhaps these responsibilities were more than he could manage, for he lost the Clerkship in 1391.

From now till the end of his life, in spite of an increased pension, he was never financially secure. His wife had died some years earlier, when their son 'little Lowis' was still a child. His last poems tell of the sadness of growing old, of the loss of poetic powers, of illness and disillusionment, though he seems to have met these blows with courage and acceptance. He never finished *The Canterbury Tales.* On 25 October 1400, he died in the house he leased in the grounds of Westminster Abbey. He was buried in the Abbey, in the first of those tombs which are grouped together in Poets' Corner.

THE CANTERBURY TALES

IT may seem surprising that so busy a public figure, with so many responsibilities, had the time or inclination for writing poetry. Chaucer was no recluse; he never lived apart from his fellows. He enjoyed their company and, as the Prologue to the Tales shows, they were the inspiration for all his writing. The Prologue is a reflection of the nation as it was in his day. There is the honourable knight, the capable but dishonest bailiff, the jolly wife of Bath, the shrewd doctor, the conscientious parson, the foul-mouthed miller, the roguish pardoner doing a brisk trade in saints' bones – or rather pigs' bones, as he admits they are. Prioress, monk, merchant, cook, judge – they come from all sections of society. Young and old, rich and poor, all shapes and sizes, opinions and temperaments, they are all here, and a very lively gathering too.

The idea of bringing them together on a pilgrimage was

Chaucer's own. It made a simple but effective framework for a wide range of stories. And what better opportunity was there than a pilgrimage to the shrine of St Thomas à Becket at Canterbury? The road was muddy and full of pot-holes, and the 56-mile journey from London took four or five days. But there were inns at convenient intervals along the way, and listening to stories would help to pass the time.

It was more than two centuries since Thomas à Becket was Archbishop of Canterbury and Chancellor of all England. Yet the pilgrims still came. Everyone remembered how Becket had quarrelled with the King. 'Who will free me from this turbulent priest?' Henry II, across the Channel in France, had bitterly cried out. Four knights, interpreting his angry words as a royal command, had set sail for England, burst into the cathedral and murdered the Archbishop in the middle of a service. The martyr's blood was soon reported to effect miraculous cures, and people came from all over England and the continent for a small leaden bottle of it – much diluted by Chaucer's day. By then the pilgrimage had become more like a merry holiday than a religious exercise. Only the parson, the humble ploughman and the honourable knight took it wholly seriously. With Harry Bailey as genial host and guide, it had become more like a modern coach tour with a lively courier in charge.

Very few of the tales the pilgrims tell are Chaucer's own invention. A fourteenth-century story-teller was not expected to invent his own story, but to tell one he liked and remembered, enlivening it with his own touches as he chose. And this Chaucer certainly did. There was no question of plagiarism. A contemporary author would have been pleased to know that his work was reaching a wider audience. The stories too were written to be read aloud. In the days before printing, books were laboriously copied out by hand, mostly by monks, and very expensive to buy.

The Oxford Scholar's library of twenty books must have cost about as much as several houses. As yet there was no tradition of silent reading to oneself. This did not come till much later in history. Chaucer, though he did not make up his stories and poems as he spoke, often read them aloud to an audience.

The tales – romances, folk tales, fables – came from all over Europe. *Prisoners of War*, adapted from the Italian poet Boccaccio, is a romantic story of chivalry and honour, of obvious appeal to the knight. *The Queen's Riddle* is an Arthurian fairy tale. Stories that made a definite point or conveyed a moral were specially popular. 'Beware of flattery' is the message of *The Cock and the Fox. In Search of Death* teaches that greed is the root of all evil, and *The White Crow* that it is unwise to interfere in others' love affairs. Many tales are based on such universal themes as human suffering, the need for loyalty and truthfulness, and the values that men should live by.

If Chaucer had written all the stories that he intended to, there would have been at least 124. But he lived to complete only 24, and some of these are only fragments. I have selected some of the best. Omitting the rhetoric and digressions that a medieval audience expected but most people find tedious today, I have retold the tales in prose as straightforwardly as I could. I have kept the Prologue in verse, using Chaucer's own metre. For the sake of variety and to suggest stages on a journey, I have split it up into sections. Each tale is introduced by Chaucer's description of the pilgrim who relates it.

Finally, a word about Chaucer's language. He wrote the stories in Middle English, most of them in the same metre as the Prologue, the five foot rhyming heroic couplet. Middle English is the name given to the language as spoken between the end of the Old English period (*c.* 1100–1150) and about 1500, when the period of modern English begins. Once you get used to it, Chaucer's language is not difficult to read. But, as you will see in the passage that follows, some words have passed out of use altogether (*ferne halwes*), and others have altered their meaning (*fowles*). Changes in pronunciation have played havoc with the rhyming. The final -e, for instance, in words like *soote* (sweet), *rote* (root) or *y-ronne* (run) is pronounced, it is not silent. Here are the opening lines of the Prologue as Chaucer wrote them:

> Whan that Aprille with his shoures soote
> The droghte of Marche hath perced to the rote,
> And bathed every veyne in swich licour,
> Of which vertu engendred is the flour;
> Whan Zephirus eek with his swete breeth
> Inspired hath in every holt and heeth
> The tendre croppes, and the yonge sonne
> Hath in the Ram his halfe cours y-ronne,
> And smale fowles maken melodye,
> That slepen al the night with open ye
> (So priketh hem nature in hir corages);
> Than longen folk to goon on pilgrimages
> (And palmers for to seken straunge strondes)
> To ferne halwes, couthe in sondry londes;
> And specially, from every shires ende
> Of Engelond, to Caunterbury they wende,
> The holy blisful martir for to seke,
> That hem hath holpen whan that they were seke.

If you'd like to know what that means, read on.

The Road to Canterbury

WHEN April's gentle showers pierce to the root
The drought of March, and seeds begin to shoot;
And every vein is filled with flowing power
To quicken the early undeveloped flower;
When Zephyr, the west wind, with sweetest breath
Blows new life on every holt and heath
Into the tender crops, and the stripling sun
Half way through the month his course has run;
When little birds, that sleep with open eye
All through the night, make joyful melody
As nature moves them and the spirit urges;
Then people long to go on pilgrimages,
And palmers long to visit foreign strands
And hallowed places known in distant lands;
From every English county, mostly they
To Kent and Canterbury make their way,
To seek St Thomas, holy martyr blessed,
Who helped them when in sickness and distressed.

It happened at this time of year one day
At the Tabard Inn in Southwark I did stay,
Ready on my pilgrimage to start
For Canterbury, with pure and eager heart.
At night there came into that hostelry
Some nine-and-twenty in a company,
Of various sorts, arrived by chance together,
Pilgrims all and birds of the same feather,
Intending toward Canterbury to ride.
The rooms were spacious and the stables wide;
The attention we received was of the best.
And shortly, when the sun had gone to rest,
I had come to know them all; we planned next day
To rise at dawn and start upon our way.

I'll tell you how we amused ourselves that night.
Our Host he welcomed us with great delight
And sat us down at table. The food and drink
Were excellent, and he himself, I'd think,
Fit to be a marshal in a hall.
He was a jovial fellow, big and tall,
With twinkling eyes, outspoken, yet full of tact;
There was no manly quality he lacked.
After supper, when our bills were paid,
'Now, ladies and gentlemen,' he said,
'– And on my honour I'm telling you no lie –
This year I've seen no jollier company
Than you, who are staying in this tavern now.
I'd like to entertain you, if I knew how.
To make the road to Canterbury seem short,
May I suggest a game to give you sport
And cost you nothing? Let each of you, I say,
Tell two stories on the outward way,
Two more returning. Whoever tells the best
Shall have his supper paid for by the rest,
Here, under my roof. I'll gladly ride

With you at my own expense and be your guide.
Tell me quickly then, do you agree?'
Gladly we agreed and asked that he
Should judge our stories and fix the dinner price.
We undertook to be ruled by his advice.
Then more wine was sent for, whereupon
After we'd drunk, to bed went everyone
Without a moment's tarrying or delay.

Next morning, at the earliest peep of day,
Up rose our Host, as prompt as crowing cock,
And gathered us together in a flock.
Then off we rode, about at walking pace
Until we reached St Thomas's watering-place.
There he reined his horse. 'Before we ride
Further,' he said, 'by lots we must decide
Who shall be the first to tell his tale.
I swear – as I hope to drink good wine and ale –
If anyone my ruling disobeys,
The expenses of our pilgrimage he pays.
Come near, my lady Prioress, and look . . .
And you, Sir Knight . . . Scholar, lay down your book . . .
Here are the lots. Who pulls the shortest straw
Is first to start. Stretch out your hands, and draw!'

They drew the straws. To everyone's delight,
By fate or chance the lot fell to the Knight.
Resigned, he said, 'Since I'm to start the game,
I accept this stroke of fortune in God's name.'

Before each tale I think it only fair
To tell you briefly who these pilgrims were,
Their rank, professions, the clothes they were riding in;
Therefore with the Knight I will begin.

The Knight

THERE was a Knight, a most illustrious man,
Who, from the moment that he first began
To ride abroad, had worshipped chivalry,
Fair dealing, honour, truth and courtesy.
He'd won distinction in his sovereign's war;
Moreover he had ridden – none so far –
Through Christendom and heathen lands as well.
He was at Alexandria when it fell;
He'd held the seat of honour when in Prussia,
Campaigned in Lithuania and in Russia.
In fifteen deadly battles he had been,
And battled for the Faith at Tramissene.
In all he undertook he won the prize.
Respected highly, he was also wise
And in behaviour modest as a maid.
Never a discourteous word he'd said
In all his life, to injure or to slight;
He was a true and perfect, noble knight.

He had good horses, but was not finely dressed;
Rust marks from his armour stained his vest.
Just home from foreign service, he had sworn
To make this pilgrimage on his return.

'Ride on,' he said, 'and listen to all I say.'
He began his tale. We rode off on our way.

Prisoners of War

THE KNIGHT'S TALE

I. A HEAP OF BODIES

LONG ago, as the old stories tell us, there lived a duke called Theseus. He was ruler of Athens and in his time the greatest conqueror under the sun.

One day, as he was riding home, he saw a company of ladies kneeling in the road and weeping bitterly. He stopped and asked them who they were.

'I was Queen of Thebes once,' said the eldest of them. 'All of us were ladies of position there.'

'What happened then, and why are you dressed in black?'

'Our enemy Creon seized the city, killed our husbands and left their bodies for the dogs to feed on. He refused to let us bury them. Oh, take pity on us, sir, and may our sorrow sink into your heart.'

This cruel injustice so enraged Theseus that he promised vengeance. With the red image of Mars, god of war, shining on his banner, he led his army to Thebes, killed Creon, and put the enemy to flight. Then he restored to the ladies the bones of their dead husbands and allowed them decent burial.

Now it happened that in the heap of Theban dead the heralds found two young knights, named Palamon and Arcite, lying side by side.

'They are cousins and belong to the royal house of Thebes,' said one of the heralds, who had recognized their coats-of-arms.

Another herald was kneeling beside them. 'They are still breathing,' he said. 'but badly wounded.'

The heralds carried them gently to the tent of Theseus. He refused to have the knights ransomed but had them taken back to Athens as prisoners of war. Here he shut them up in a room at the top of a tower.

And here they stayed as the months and the years dragged on.

One May morning soon after sunrise Palamon looked out of the iron-barred window and saw a beautiful girl, with a plaited tress of yellow hair a yard long, in the garden far below. It was Emily, Theseus' young sister-in-law. Lovelier than a lily on its green stalk, fresher than the blossoms of early summer, she was picking flowers to make a garland. As she walked she sang, and her voice was like an angel's in heaven.

Suddenly Palamon fell back with a cry.

'Why did you cry out?' said Arcite. 'Because we're prisoners? There's nothing we can do about that except endure it.'

'No, it's not that. It was the sight of that girl – it pierced me to the heart. Is she a woman or a goddess? I think she must be Venus.' He knelt down and prayed. 'Venus, if it is you – oh, help us to escape from prison. Or if we must stay here for ever, have pity on us.'

Then Arcite looked out of the window. When he saw the girl, he too was pierced to the heart. 'If I cannot win her favour, I shall die,' he said.

'Are you joking?'

'I am perfectly serious.'

'Have you forgotten the solemn promises we made, never to cross each other in love or anything else?' cried Palamon angrily. 'You traitor! I loved her first.'

'Nonsense. I loved her before you. You couldn't even tell if she was a woman or a goddess. Your love is spiritual, mine is love for a human being. . . But what's the use of quarrelling? We're both prisoners, condemned to lie here for ever. No hope of a ransom, no hope of marriage either. Someone else will win her. We're like two dogs that fought all day over a bone – then a kite swooped down and took it. Love her if you must, but I shall love her too, and that's that.'

So began a long and bitter quarrel.

In the end a friend of Theseus, who also knew Arcite, came to Athens and persuaded the Duke to free Arcite without ransom. Theseus agreed on condition that Arcite never returned to Athens again. 'If you ever show your face in any land of mine again, I'll have you beheaded,' he said.

So Arcite returned to Thebes – far from happily, for although he was free he would probably never see Emily again. 'You're the winner, Palamon,' he reflected. 'You may be still in prison, but you can see Emily and that turns prison into paradise. I live in exile, beyond help or hope.'

Palamon was just as envious of his cousin. 'You're free to walk in Thebes as you wish,' he thought. 'You can raise an army, make war on Athens, win Emily for your wife. Here am I, dying in a cage. Oh yes, you've come off best, Arcite.' And his face was grey and lifeless as cold ashes.

Summer passed, and the long winter nights doubled the torments of both. Who can say which of them suffered more – the prisoner in his chains or the free man who could never see Emily again?

2. LIKE WILD BOARS FROTHING WHITE FOAM

Back again in Thebes, Arcite missed Emily so much that he could not sleep or eat. Hollow-eyed and grey-faced, he grew thin and dry as a stick and shunned all company. The sound of music made him burst into tears, and his spirits were so low that all he could do was mope around and mumble. Love had turned him upside down.

One night, a year or two later, he had a dream about the winged god Mercury. 'Cheer up, Arcite,' said the god. 'If you want to see the end of your troubles, go to Athens.'

Startled, Arcite woke, got out of bed and looked into a mirror. His sufferings had so much changed his appearance that he hardly recognized himself. 'If I can't recognize myself, it's unlikely that anyone else will recognize me either,' he thought. 'I'll change my clothes, go to Athens and see my lady every day.'

So he dressed as a labourer and went to Athens, where he got a job in Emily's household, giving his name as Philostrate. Being young, tall and strong, he was able to cut wood, draw water, and do anything required of him. For a year or two he worked as Emily's page. Courteous as well as useful, he became so popular that Theseus promoted him to his own household and made him his personal chamberlain, paying him well. Here he worked for three years, and there was no one that Theseus regarded more highly.

Meanwhile for seven long years Palamon had pined away in the dreadful darkness of his prison. Then one night – soon after midnight on the third of May – with a friend's help he drugged his jailer's wine, broke out of prison and fled from the city. At dawn he was hiding in a wood, intending to stay there all day and after dark go on to Thebes and raise an army to attack Theseus.

And where was Arcite, this same May morning? As the busy lark, messenger of day, was greeting the rising sun, he looked out of his bedroom window. The east began to laugh with light, and the sun to dry the silver drops of dew on the leaves. He leapt on to his horse and rode out into the fields, to do homage to the month of May.

A mile or two out of the city he came to the wood where Palamon was hiding. As he made himself a garland of honeysuckle and hawthorn leaves, he sang:

> May, with all your flowers and green,
> Welcome, welcome, fair fresh May,
> I'll pick you something green today.

He leaped down joyfully from his horse and walked along a path between the trees, past the very bush where Palamon was hiding, terrified of being spotted and quite unaware that it was Arcite singing. Nor had Arcite any idea that his cousin was so close.

Tired of walking, Arcite stopped singing and his mood changed. Lovers' moods are for ever changing; now high up in the tree-tops, now down among the brambles, they go up and down like a bucket in a well. With a sigh he sat down and spoke his troubled thoughts aloud: 'In my city all is sorrow and confusion. Though I have the royal blood of Thebes in my veins, yet I am the slave of Theseus, my mortal enemy. I'm now called Philostrate and dare not use my own name. Wretched Palamon wastes away in prison. Worse still, I am dying for love of Emily.'

Palamon felt as if a cold sword had slid through his heart. Shaking with anger, he sprang out of the bushes, his face deadly pale, and shouted, 'I've caught you now, traitor. So you've fooled Theseus by changing your name. I am Palamon, your enemy. You must give up your love for Emily or I'll kill you.'

Fierce as a lion, Arcite drew his sword. But when he saw that Palamon was unarmed, he held back. 'I'll fight you here tomorrow, in secret,' he said. 'Tonight I'll bring you meat and drink and bedding, and tomorrow armour for us both – you can choose the best for yourself. If you kill me and win Emily, then you may have her.'

Palamon agreed and they parted. Arcite rode back to the city. Next morning at daybreak he returned with the armour. Without a word they helped each other to arm, then fell to it like a lion and a tiger, or like wild boars frothing white foam. They fought till they were ankle-deep in blood.

Now it happened that Theseus, a keen huntsman, had chosen this very morning to go hunting with Queen Hippolyta and Emily. He had been told that there was a stag in this part of the wood. Shading his eyes against the sun, he saw not a stag but Palamon and Arcite fighting, their bright swords flashing so fast that it seemed the slightest stroke was enough to fell an oak. But he had no idea who they were. Spurring his horse, he dashed between them, then drew his sword and cried, 'Stop! The first to strike another blow shall die.' And he asked them who they were and why they were fighting.

'Sir, we both deserve to die,' said Palamon. 'We are your prisoners. Our lives are a burden to us. We do not ask for mercy. Please kill me first, and then my friend – or kill him first, if you prefer.'

'But who is he? You haven't told me his name.'

'You know him as Philostrate, the false name he assumed when he entered your palace and soon became your chief squire. He has fooled you for years. His real name is Arcite.'

'Arcite? But I banished him from my country.'

'Well, now he's back again because he loves Emily.'

'And who are you, so glib with your accusations?' said Theseus angrily.

'I am your enemy Palamon and your prisoner till yesterday when I escaped. I too love Emily – so fiercely that I am ready to die now in her sight. But you must kill us both, my cousin too.'

'You are condemned by your own confession,' said Theseus. 'By red almighty Mars, you shall die.'

The Queen and Emily, who with all the other ladies in the party had been sitting on their horses listening in amazement to all this, began to weep. They were full of pity for these two noble knights – for love alone was the cause of their quarrel. When they saw their red and gaping wounds, they leaped from their horses and went down on their knees and begged Theseus for their lives.

At first he shook with anger, but gradually, as he pondered the case of the two knights, he relented. Here they were, with their lives in his hands, and both prepared to die. And he began to make excuses for them. They had behaved foolishly, but anyone in love would try to escape from prison if he could. Look at the state they were in now – was there any bigger fool than a lover? The funniest thing of all was that Emily, the cause of all this silliness, knew no more about the matter than a cuckoo or a hare. And he said to the two knights, 'I know from my own experience what the pangs of love are like and how violently they affect a man. The Queen, who is kneeling here, and my dear sister Emily have asked me to pardon you. I will gladly do so. But first you must promise never to make war on my country again.'

They swore the oath and he pardoned them.

'My sister Emily can't marry you both,' he said. 'I propose to free you, but fifty weeks from today you must return here, each with a hundred knights armed for a tournament. I shall build the lists, judge the tournament myself and give Emily to the winner. Do you agree?'

Delighted with Theseus' generosity, they agreed at once. Full of hope, they rode back home to the ancient walls of Thebes.

3. THE BUILDING OF THE LISTS

The lists that Theseus built were the finest in the world. Circular in shape, with stone walls and tiers of seats rising to sixty feet, they were a mile round, with a gate of white marble at each end. Above the east gate he built a chapel to Venus, goddess of love, and above the west gate one to Mars, god of battle. In a turret on the north wall he made a chapel of white alabaster and red coral in honour of Diana, goddess of chastity.

The walls of the chapel of Venus were painted with stories of great lovers of the past. There was also a statue of the goddess, who seemed to be afloat on green waves that glittered like glass. On her head she had a garland of fresh roses. The paintings in the chapel of red Mars were of dark and wintry forests – you could almost hear the stormy winds blowing. And there were scenes of treachery and terror and cruel murder. The armed statue of Mars stood in a cart, grim-faced, his red eyes glaring, and there was a wolf at his feet. In Diana's chapel the paintings were of hunting scenes. The statue of the goddess was dressed in green; she had a bow in her hand and a quiverful of arrows. All these marvels were the work of the finest sculptors, painters, craftsmen and builders in the land.

The day for the tournament approached, when Palamon and Arcite were due to return, each with a hundred knights, to settle the claim to Emily. They arrived in good time, each wearing the armour he liked best – a coat of mail, or breast-plate and tunic, or plated body-armour. Some carried a Prussian shield, a battle-axe or steel mace.

With Palamon came Lycurgus, the great black-bearded

King of Thrace. Under his bushy brows glared his eyes, yellowy-red. Broad-shouldered, tough-limbed, with long powerful arms, he wore over his armour a coal-black bear-skin. Black as a raven's feathers were his beard and long hair. His chariot and the chair he sat in were made of gold. So too was the crown he wore, which was set with rubies and diamonds. A hundred noblemen, stout-hearted and fully armed, followed behind.

With Arcite came Emetrius, King of India. Astride a bay horse with trappings of steel and cloth of gold, he looked like Mars, the god of war. His coat-of-arms was of cloth of Tartary studded with white pearls, his saddle of beaten gold; and his cloak sparkled with rubies. The ringlets of his crisp fair hair shone in the sun, and his voice rang out like the thunder of trumpets. On his head he wore a wreath of green laurel, and he carried on his hand a white eagle. While tame lions and leopards gambolled round his horse, a hundred noblemen followed.

In this way Palamon and Arcite and their companies of nobles entered Athens. And Theseus feasted them and did them honour.

That Sunday night, two hours before dawn, Palamon heard the lark begin to sing. He went straight to the temple of Venus in the lists, then knelt down and prayed:

'Lady Venus, fairest of the fair, have pity on my bitter tears, and take my humble prayer to your heart. I am not asking for victory or fame, but only to win Emily, to have her in my arms. Though Mars is the god of war, you are the goddess of love, and your power is as great as his. If I win, I shall worship for ever at your altar. If this is not your will, let Arcite tomorrow run me through the heart with his spear. I shall not mind if he is the winner, for I shall be dead.'

He made a sacrifice to Venus. When her statue trembled, Palamon took this to mean that his prayer had been granted.

At sunrise on the same day Emily got up and hurried with her maids to the temple of Diana. As the smoke from their sacrifice rose into the air, she washed her body in well-water. But I won't describe that now – it's better to leave it to the imagination.

She kindled two fires on the altar, then prayed to Diana: 'Chaste goddess of the green woods, Queen of Pluto's dark kingdom, you know that I have no wish to be married. I am one of your followers, for I love hunting and walking in the wild woods, and men and children mean nothing to me. Send peace and friendship between Palamon and Arcite, who love me so much, and make them forget me. Turn their hearts and tormenting love away from me. But if you will not grant me this, give me to the one who loves me most.'

Suddenly a strange thing happened. One of the altar fires went out, then blazed up again. With a whistling sound – like the sound of wet branches burning – the other fire went out, and drops of blood oozed out of the ends of the branches.

Emily shrieked with terror and began to weep. Then Diana herself appeared, bow in hand and dressed like a hunter.

'Dry your tears, daughter,' she said. 'The gods have decided that you must marry one of these two men, but I may not tell you which.'

The arrows in her quiver clattered together and she vanished. Emily hurried home, wondering what all this could mean.

An hour later Arcite went to the temple of Mars, the fierce god of war, to sacrifice.

'Strong god,' he prayed, 'accept my sacrifice. Help me in battle tomorrow and give me victory. I will hang my banner in your temple and keep your altar fire burning till the day I die.'

The rings that hung from the temple doors clattered loudly, startling Arcite. As the altar fires blazed up and a sweet smell rose from the ground, Arcite threw more incense into the flame. The coat of mail on the statue of Mars rang, and a low soft voice murmured 'Victory!'

Greatly cheered and full of hope, Arcite returned to his lodging, as happy as a bird in the sun.

Thanks to the granting of these two seemingly contradictory promises, there was a great uproar in heaven, and Jupiter tried hard to pacify his gods and goddesses. It was wise old Saturn who found a solution.

'Don't be upset, my dear daughter,' he said to Venus. 'I have some power to control events. I shall do my best to see that your knight shall have his lady. Now dry your tears, my dear. I will not disappoint you.'

'What about me?' said Mars gruffly.

'You shall help your knight as well,' Saturn replied.

4. THE GREAT TOURNAMENT

That day there was a great festival in Athens. After all the dancing and jousting, people went to bed early, as they wanted to be up next morning in time to watch the tournament.

At daybreak what a scene it was! The clatter of horses and armour in the inn yards; lords riding to the palace on stallions and palfreys; rich armour cunningly wrought by the goldsmith; bright shields, gold helmets, head-pieces and trappings, breast-plates and coats-of-arms; squires fixing spearheads, buckling on helmets, strapping shields with lacings of thong – bustle and activity everywhere. There were foam-flecked steeds gnawing gold bridles; armourers running this way and that with files and hammers; yeomen on foot, crowds of common people armed with short sticks; pipes, trumpets, kettledrums, clarions blasting for battle; the palace choked with groups arguing about the two Theban knights and which side would win. 'I fancy Black-beard' – 'Bald-head's my man' – 'No, that fellow with hair like a haystack' – 'Ah, here's a winner – his battle-axe weighs twenty pounds!' And so it went on, long after the sun was up.

Great Theseus, woken by the music and the din, stayed in his room till the two Theban knights arrived. Then he went to the palace window and sat there, enthroned like a god. From a scaffold a herald shouted for silence and announced the rules of the contest:

'Because there is so much noble blood here, the Duke wishes no one to be killed. He therefore modifies his original conditions. He forbids the use in the lists of darts, pole-axes, or short stabbing swords with sharp points. No one may ride more than one course against his opponent, dismounting to parry only in self-defence. The loser of each encounter shall be taken prisoner, not killed, and must be brought to the stake at either end of the lists. Should the leader o either side be captured or kill his opponent, the tournament will end at once. Good luck to you now.'

There were cheers and shouts of 'God bless the Duke!' then a fanfare of trumpets as the whole company rode off through the city, with Theseus, his queen, Emily, and the two Thebans leading the way.

And so they came to the lists.

When all had taken their seats, with Theseus and his party in the place of honour, the two companies entered. Arcite, with a red banner and his hundred knights, entered from the west through the Mars gate. Palamon, with a white banner and his hundred knights, entered from the east through the Venus gate. All the names were called (to prevent cheating) and the gates were shut. The heralds withdrew, and the tournament began.

And what a contest it was! With spears at the ready both companies, spurring their horses, charged and clashed. Up sprang the spears, twenty feet into the air; out flashed the swords, bright as silver. Helmets were hacked to pieces, bones smashed by huge maces, with blood spurting everywhere. One man hacked a path through the thickest of the fray where even the strongest horse stumbled. Another rolled like a ball underfoot, then sprang to his feet and with the truncheon of his spear hurtled a rider and his horse to the ground. Another was wounded, taken prisoner and dragged still fighting to the stake, where because of the rules he had to stay.

Palamon and Arcite met and wounded each other several times in the course of the day. Arcite fought like a tiger that has lost its cub, Palamon like a lion ravenous for blood. Twice each unhorsed the other. Before the sun went down, King Emetrius seized Palamon, who was fighting Arcite, and sank his sword deep into his flesh. Palamon refused to yield, and it took twenty men to drag him to the stake. King Lycurgus was struck down while trying to rescue him. Before Palamon was captured, he knocked King Emetrius a sword's length out of his saddle. But it didn't save Palamon from being dragged still resisting to the stake, and there he had to stay.

When Theseus saw this, he stopped the fight. 'It's all over,' he said. 'Arcite shall have Emily. He has won her fairly.'

So loud was the joyful shout that rose from the crowd that it's a wonder that the lists didn't collapse.

But Venus up above wasn't pleased. 'I have been put to shame,' said the Queen of Love, and she wept enough tears to fill the lists.

'Hush, daughter. Be patient,' said Saturn. 'Mars has had his way, but soon you will have yours.'

Trumpets blared, heralds shouted. Arcite took off his helmet and rode along the lists to show his face. As he looked up towards Emily, she smiled down at him. Women usually like a winner.

Suddenly a fury sprang out of the ground. It was sent by Pluto, King of the Underworld, at Saturn's request. The frightened horse reared and swerved, and Arcite was thrown violently against the pommel of his saddle, crushing his chest. He fell to the ground and lay still, with the dark blood streaming down his face. He was carried sadly away to Theseus' palace, where they cut him out of his armour and laid him on a bed, still alive and crying all the time for Emily.

Medicine was no use to Arcite's injury. As the poison spread and his chest became swollen, it quickly grew worse. Arcite knew he was dying. He sent for Emily and his cousin Palamon and said, 'Good-bye, dear Emily. Mere words cannot express my sorrow. I love you with all my heart – and have to leave you. What is this world? What does man ask to have? Now with his love, now in his cold grave, alone and friendless! Good-bye, Emily, my sweet enemy. Take me in your arms, listen to what I'm saying. Because of my jealous love for you I have for a long time quarrelled with Palamon. I know of no one who deserves your love more than he. If you ever choose to marry, remember Palamon.'

His speech began to fail, and the cold of death crept up from his feet and spread through his body. His breath was short, his eyes darkened, but still he gazed at Emily. His last words were, 'Mercy . . . Emily!'

Then his spirit left his body. Where did it go? As I've never been there myself, I really can't say, so I'll keep my mouth shut. Anyhow, I'm no theologian.

Emily burst into tears, and Theseus came and gently led her away. In his great grief his old father Aegeus did his best to comfort him. 'Everyone must die', he said. 'This world is but a thoroughfare of sorrow, and we are pilgrims passing to and fro. Death is the end of every worldly trouble.'

Theseus now considered where to build the funeral pyre. He decided that the best place was the wood where Arcite and Palamon had first fought each other, and he gave orders for the ancient oaks to be cut down and prepared for burning.

So the trees were felled: as well as oak there were birch, willow, chestnut, ash, lime, maple, yew and many other kinds. As the trees crashed down, animals and birds fled in panic; and ground now bare, which had never seen bright sun before, went pale with fear. Nymphs and fauns and other woodland gods who had lost their peaceful tree homes were running everywhere.

Great was the labour in the building of the pyre. First, many loads of straw were put down; then boughs and branches reaching twenty fathoms wide at the base, but tapering upwards to the point where the green summit reached into the sky.

Theseus had a coffin prepared. He laid Arcite inside, robed in cloth of gold, with a crown of green laurel on his head and a shining sword in his hand. On the day of the funeral the noblest Greeks carried it on their shoulders with slow steps through the streets of the city, their eyes red and wet with tears. Three white horses, with trappings of glittering steel, followed. On each sat a rider, the first carrying Arcite's shield, the second his spear, and the third his Turkish bow. On the right walked old Aegeus, and on the left Theseus. In their hands they carried fine gold vessels, full of honey and milk and blood and wine. Next came Palamon, with ashes in his hair and black clothes wet with tears; then Emily, according to custom carrying the funeral torch. She was the saddest in the whole company. So they came through the city and out into the country to the funeral pyre.

When they had laid the coffin in the pyre, with treasures all round it, Emily thrust the lighted torch into the timber, and quickly the flames took hold. Some threw shields, some threw spears, some threw the clothes they were wearing, and cups full of wine and milk and blood into the fire. A band of Greeks rode three times round it with loud shouting, then three times again rattling their spears. Three times the ladies broke into crying. In all the noise and smoke and choking heat, Emily fainted and was taken home to Athens. But Arcite was burnt to cold ashes.

The mourning went on for a very long time, but at last it ended. Then Theseus sent for Palamon and Emily and brought them before the assembled council. When all voices were hushed, he spoke quietly to them out of the wisdom of his heart:

'He who in the beginning created all things decided that nothing should endure for ever. Even the oak tree, that grows so slowly and lives so long, at last decays; the stone we tread on wears away; the broad river sometimes dries up; great cities decline, and all things have an end. Everyone must die, the king as well as his page.

'Therefore it is wise, it seems to me, to make a virtue of necessity, to accept cheerfully what is common to us all and cannot be avoided. The most highly honoured man is the one who dies in the flower of his excellence, when he is sure of his good name. Why should we grieve when Arcite, the flower of chivalry, has departed with honour from the foul prison of this life? Why should his cousin and his wife here grudge him his happiness?

'So I say then that the time has come for us to be merry, and that we should thank Jupiter for all his goodness. Let us now out of our two sorrows make one perfect joy.'

He turned to Emily and said, 'Sister, this is my opinion, and my council here are agreed to it, that you should take Palamon for your husband and lord. He is your own knight. He has suffered for you and served you with all his heart; he deserves your compassion. Give me your hand.'

Then he turned to Palamon and said, 'I don't think you will have any objection. Come here and take your lady by the hand.'

So the bond of marriage was made between them and confirmed by all the council present. With joyful song Emily and Palamon were wedded. May God, who made the wide world, bless his love – he paid dearly for it.

All went well with Palamon. He lived in health, wealth and happiness. Emily loved him so tenderly and served him so nobly that never a word of jealousy passed between them.

That is the end of my story. God bless you all.

The Squire

A SQUIRE rode with the Knight – this was his son,
Who not yet his knighthood spurs had won.
His locks were curly, as though they had been pressed;
Some twenty years of age he was, I guessed,
A fiery lover too, of middling height,
Strong of limb and wonderfully light.
On many a raid he'd served with cavalry
In Flanders and Artois and Picardy
Where, in so short a time, his brave behaviour
He fondly hoped would win his lady's favour.
He was embroidered like a field alight
And glowing with fresh flowers, red and white.
He liked to sing or play the flute all day;
He was as fresh as is the month of May.
His gown was short, the sleeves were long and wide;
He knew how to sit his horse and how to ride.
Poet he was, composer, and, what's more,
Could dance, joust in the lists, and write and draw.

So passionate his love, till dark grew pale
He slept no more than does a nightingale.
Courteous, modest, willing, as well as able,
He carved before his father at the table.

The Yeoman

THE Squire had only a Yeoman at his side,
For that was always how he chose to ride,
The Yeoman clad in coat and hood of green.
Some peacock-feathered arrows, bright and keen,
Below his belt were sheathed, all neat and trim
(In caring for them few could equal him;
His arrows never drooped, with feathers low),
And in his hand he held a mighty bow.
His hair was cropped, he had a brown complexion,
And knew the art of woodcraft to perfection.
To stop the string from rubbing, he wore a guard
Of leather on his arm. A shield and sword
Hung at one side; the other was equipped
With a gaily mounted dagger, sharply tipped.
A silver badge of St Christopher was worn
To keep him safe, and at his belt a horn.
He really was a forester, I'd guess.

The Prioress

THERE also was a nun, a Prioress,
Who smiled most sweetly. She was shy and coy;
Her greatest oath was only 'By St Loy!'
(He was a goldsmith and a handsome boy),
And she was known as Madam Eglantine.
In church she sang through her nose; her French was
　　divine,
As taught by nuns at Stratford-atte-Bow –
The language Frenchmen speak she did not know.
Her table manners were exceptional;
No morsel did she from her lips let fall
To drop upon her bosom, and of course
She never dipped her fingers in the sauce.
Her upper lip she always wiped so clean
That on her cup no spot of grease was seen;
She never grabbed a dish, but reached sedately;
Her face was pleasant, her demeanour stately.
So kind was she, it made her overwrought
And tearful if she saw a mouse caught
In a trap, or if it were dead, or hurt and bleeding.

She kept some lapdogs she was always feeding
With meat and milk or the most expensive bread.
Her tears fell thick and fast if one were dead,
Or someone fetched a stick and made it smart –
She was all sympathy and tender heart.
Her nose was finely shaped, her eyes glass-grey,
Her red mouth soft and small; but I'm sorry to say
She wore her wimple – against the Bishop's order –
High on her head, with a dainty pleated border;
And, though an exposed forehead he'd not allow,
It stretched almost a span from brow to brow.
Her cloak, I noticed, was the latest fashion;
To judge from her coral beads, she had a passion
For jewellery and trinkets, and – heaven above! –
Her brooch was carved with A for *Amor* (Love).

The Nun's Priest

'COME over here,' said the Host. 'Good Brother John,
Forget that wretched hack you're riding on.
Cheer up! I know it's gaunt, ill-groomed and lean,
But if it will go you needn't care a bean.
So tell us a tale, to prove your merry heart.'
'All right,' said the kindly priest. 'I'm ready to start.'

The Cock and the Fox

THE NUN'S PRIEST'S TALE

ONCE there was a poor widow, who was getting on in years. She lived in a small cottage in a valley beside a clump of trees. Ever since the day she was last a wife, she had lived a very patient, simple life, for she had few belongings and not much money. She kept herself and her two daughters by managing as best she could with what God sent her. She had three large sows, no more, three cows, and a sheep called Molly. Her kitchen living room, in which she ate her frugal meals, was smoky and dark with soot – there was no chimney. She didn't need hotly spiced sauces, no dainty morsels travelled down her throat; her food was as plain as her dress, and as she never ate too much, she always kept well. A modest diet, hard exercise and a contented mind were her only medicine. She never suffered from gout to stop her dancing, and was never troubled with giddiness. She drank neither white nor red wine, but had plenty of milk and brown bread, grilled bacon and sometimes an egg or two. She was in fact a kind of dairy-woman.

She had a yard fenced round with sticks, and there was a dry ditch outside. Here she used to keep a cock called Chanticleer. No cock in the whole country could crow as he did. His voice was merrier than the merry organ that's played in church on Mass days. He crowed exactly on the hour, for he knew the time by instinct and was more regular than a clock. His comb was redder than fine coral and battlemented like a castle wall; his black bill shone like jet; his legs and toes were sky-blue, with nails whiter than a lily; his feathered coat was the colour of burnished gold.

This noble cock had seven hens to delight him. They were his sisters and his wives, remarkably like him in colour, and the loveliest of them all – the one with the fairest colours on her throat – was called Madam Partlet. She was courteous, tactful, gracious, and good company for him; and she had such dainty ways that ever since she was a week old she had quite won his heart. Chanticleer was head over heels in love with her. What a pleasure it was, when the bright sun rose, to hear them singing together in harmony 'My love has gone away'. For in those days, I'm told, animals and birds could talk and sing.

Early one morning, as Chanticleer was sitting on his perch in the kitchen among all his wives with Partlet beside him, he suddenly began to groan like someone having a nightmare.

Partlet was thoroughly alarmed. 'Dear heart, what ever's wrong with you?' she said. 'That's a fine way to sleep. You ought to be ashamed.'

'Please don't distress yourself, madam,' said Chanticleer.

'I've just had a ghastly dream – I can't get over it. I dreamed I was strutting up and down the yard, when suddenly I saw an animal – a sort of dog. He tried to grab hold of me and kill me. He was a yellowy-red colour, with black tips on his tail and ears. He had a tiny snout, and his eyes were burning. He frightened me to death.'

'You coward!' she cried. 'Now you've lost my heart and my love for ever. I couldn't possibly love a coward. Women like their husbands to be tough, wise, generous, dependable – not mean and boastful idiots, scared of the slightest thing. Have you no spirit to match that beard of yours? Fancy being frightened of dreams! There's nothing in them. They only come from over-eating, from noxious vapours rising from the belly. Yes, that's where they come from, all those shooting flames, those black bears and black bulls and devils straight from hell. Remember Cato, that wise Roman. Wasn't he right when he said, "Take no notice of dreams"? What you need, sir, when we fly down from our perch, is a laxative. There's no chemist in the village, but I can tell you the names of the herbs that will quickly settle you – spurge laurel, centaury, fumitory, hellebore, blackthorn berries, herb-ivy – you'll find them all growing in the yard. But before you take them you must coddle your digestion for a day or two with a light diet of worms. . . Now for goodness' sake, husband, cheer up – and take no more notice of dreams.'

'Thank you very much, madam, for your learned advice,' said the cock. 'All the same, I must point out that not all the authorities agree with Cato. Some of the old books, written by weightier men than he, say just the opposite. They show that dreams foretell the joys and sorrows that people are to meet in life, and we must pay attention to them.' And he reminded his wife of Daniel and Joseph in the Old Testament, of Pharaoh King of Egypt and his butler and baker. 'So you see, madam, dreams are portents of danger, and we must be warned by them. As for laxatives, I tell you, I don't believe in them. They're poisonous – I can't stand them.

'But let's talk of more agreeable matters. . . There's one thing, Madam Partlet, for which I'm deeply grateful to God. Whenever I look at your beautiful face – you are so scarlet red about the eyes – my fears all vanish. You know, *In principio, mulier est hominis confusio* – that's Latin, madam – it means "Woman is man's whole joy and happiness" – and I swear it's true. For at night, when I feel your soft feathers beside me – what a pity our perch is made too narrow for me to ride on you! – I'm so full of joy and comfort that I defy all dreams.'

He flew down from the beam, for it was now daylight, and all his hens followed. Finding a grain of corn in the yard, he clucked and called them to him. All his fears had vanished. He strutted up and down on his toes, fierce as a lion. Each time he found a grain of corn he clucked, and all his wives came running to him. He was like a royal prince in his palace. . . Now I'll leave him, pecking away at his food, and get on with the story.

When March, the month in which the world began, was over, Chanticleer in all his glory, with his seven wives beside him, glanced up at the bright sun. He knew instinctively that it was nine o'clock, and he gave a joyful crow.

'The sun has climbed into the sky,' he said. 'Madam Partlet, delight of my heart, listen to the birds – how happily they sing! Look at the flowers – how fresh they grow! My heart is full of merriment.'

Suddenly misfortune struck. (God knows, the joys of this world never last long.)

A cunning coal-black fox, who had been living in the copse for three years, had during the night broken through the hedge into the yard. He was hiding in a bed of cabbages, waiting his chance to fall on Chanticleer, like a murderer poised to spring. Oh treacherous assassin, lurking in your den! Oh Judas Iscariot! Oh Chanticleer, how you must curse the day that you flew down from the beam into the yard! Your dreams had warned you that this day would be a perilous one for you. I know that scholars dispute and argue about the meaning of dreams, but I can't go into all that now. My story is about a cock who took his wife's advice. She told him to walk in the yard as usual, on the day after his dream, and the result was disastrous. A woman's advice is nearly always wrong. Think what happened to Adam in the Garden of Eden – it was a woman's advice that lost him Paradise. . . But enough of that. I'm only joking and I don't wish to give offence. Remember, these are the cock's words, not my own. Personally I can see no harm in women.

To return to my story . . . Partlet was enjoying a dustbath in the sand, with all her sisters basking in the sun near by, and Chanticleer singing more merrily than a mermaid in the sea. As he cast his eye on a butterfly among the cabbages, he suddenly noticed a fox crouching there. That was the end of his crowing. 'Cock, cock!' he cried in panic, desperate to escape.

'Good sir, why do you want to run away?' said the fox quickly. 'You needn't be afraid of me. I'm your friend and wouldn't dream of spying on you or hurting you in any way. I've come to hear you sing. Your voice is as beautiful as an angel's in heaven, and you have more feeling for music than the finest musician. My lord your father (God bless him!) and your lady mother often paid me the compliment of calling at my house, and I'd like to entertain you as well. I never heard anyone except yourself, who could sing like your father. He put his whole heart into it. Standing on his toes, screwing up his eyes, stretching out his neck, he sang at the top of his voice. Now, sir, let's see if you can do as well.'

Ravished with this flattery and suspecting nothing, Chanticleer began to flap his wings. Standing on tiptoe, he stretched out his neck, closed his eyes and crowed at the top of his voice. Up sprang Master Russell the fox, grabbed him by the throat, and made off with him towards the wood.

Alas, one cannot escape fate. What a pity that Chanticleer ever flew down from the beam, and that his wife didn't believe in dreams! And all this happened on a Friday too.

Not since the fall of Troy, when Pyrrhus seized King Priam by the beard and slew him and all the Trojan women wept, was there such lamentation as the hens made now, when Chanticleer was carried off. And Madam Partlet shrieked loudest of them all.

The widow and her two daughters heard the screams. They ran out of doors just as the fox, with the cock slung over his back, was racing for the wood.

'Help! Help! A fox!' they cried, and ran after him, followed by a crowd of men with sticks, Colly the dog, Talbot, Garland, and Malkyn the maid with a distaff still in her hand. Terrified by the barking and shouting, the cow and calf and even the pigs joined in the chase. They yelled like devils in hell. They ran until they nearly burst. The bees swarmed out of the hive, the ducks squawked, the geese flew in panic over the trees. Jack Straw and his mob, when they attacked London, killing Flemings right and left, never made half such a din as this rabble chasing the fox. They came with their trumpets of brass and box-wood and horn and bone. They blew and tooted, shrieked and whooped until it seemed as if the heavens would fall.

Now listen, everyone, and hear how fortune can suddenly overthrow her enemy.

The cock, flat on the fox's back, managed in spite of his terror to cry out, 'Sir, if I were you – God help me! – I'd say to that rabble, "Go home, you country bumpkins. I've brought this cock as far as the wood, and I'm going to hang on to him, whatever your tricks. I'll eat him, right now!" '

'Good idea,' said the fox.

But the moment he opened his mouth, out flew the cock, high up into a tree.

When the fox saw that he'd lost him, 'Oh, Chanticleer,' he whined, 'it was wrong of me to frighten you just now, when I grabbed you from the yard. I'm sorry – I meant no harm. Come down, and I'll tell you what I really meant. I promise I will.'

'Oh no, you won't. You want to flatter me into singing with my eyes shut. I'm damned if I'll let you fool me like that again. I've learnt my lesson.'

'And I've learnt mine too,' said the fox. 'To keep my mouth shut.'

And that's what happens (the priest concluded) when you're silly and believe in flatterers. Good friends, take the lesson to heart. It concerns you too.

The Monk

THERE was a Monk, a handsome manly lad,
Steward to his estate, and hunting-mad,
But fit to be an abbot, he was so able.
Many a princely horse adorned his stable;
And, when he rode, his bridle bells you'd hear
Jingling in a whistling wind as clear
And loud as does the monastery bell
Where he presided, Prior of the cell.
The Rule of old St Maur and Benedict
Was out-of-date, he thought, and somewhat strict;
So ancient pious precepts went neglected,
For modern ways alone this monk respected.

Rightly, I judge, he did not care a pin
If told that hunters are unholy men
And a monk must always keep to his own cloister –
Opinions, I agree, not worth an oyster.
Why should he always with some book be saddled
And go on studying till his wits were addled,
Or toil with his hands as St Augustine bade?
I say, let St Augustine keep his spade.
He loved hard riding, did this monk all right;
His greyhounds were as swift as birds in flight,
For his dearest pleasure was to hunt the hare
Astride his horse – and no expense he'd spare.

I saw his sleeves were trimmed above the hand
With squirrel fur, the finest in the land.
To fasten up his hood below the chin,
He had a most elaborate golden pin,
That held in the larger end a lover's knot.
His eyes were bright as flames beneath a pot;
His bald head shone like a mirror, his face looked
   greased.
He was a plump and splendid-looking priest
In excellent shape, no pale tormented ghost;
A fat expensive swan was his favourite roast.
His palfrey was as brown as is a berry.

The Friar

THERE was a Friar, a lively chap and merry,
Impressive too. His tongue knew how to flatter
Nicely; he was rich in local chatter.
Within the boundaries where he begged for alms
He was well liked and on the best of terms
With wealthy squires and women with possessions,
As he was authorized to hear confessions
For graver sins than those that could be named
In front of parish priests, or so he claimed.
Easy was his penance and given sweetly
If he was sure of being tipped discreetly.

His hood was crammed with pins and pocket-knives
Inside the folds, to give to pretty wives.
His voice was pleasing, with a merry ring;
He could play the fiddle and could sing
Ballads by the score and drive you silly.
His neck, I saw, was whiter than the lily,
Though he was champion-tough. In every town
He knew the inns and taverns up and down.
To barmaids more than beggars he would come –
It didn't do to mix with common scum,
But with the rich. Where profit could be found,
Polite and humble he'd be hanging round.
For begging, no other friar could match this tout;
So pleasantly his text he trotted out
That, even if a widow had no shoes,
She'd give him sixpence rather than refuse.
He made his biggest profits on the sly.

On settling days he romped about, as spry
As a puppy; he was helpful (for a fee);
Not dressed, like cloistered scholar, shabbily,
But smartly as a Doctor or a Pope.
Of double-worsted was his outer cloak,
And rounded like a bell straight from the press.
He lisped a little, purely to impress
And make his words trip sweetly on the tongue;
And when he'd played his harp or sung his song,
His eyes would twinkle in his head, as bright
As stars in heaven on a frosty night.
The Friar's name was Hubert, so I heard.

The Merchant

THERE was a Merchant with a forking beard,
In motley dress; high on his horse he sat;
Upon his head a Flemish beaver hat;
His boots were fastened handsomely and neatly.
Impressively he spoke, and indiscreetly,
Informing you in any undertaking
Precisely how much profit he was making.
He'd give anything to have the seas kept clear
Of pirate ship and coastal privateer.
Bargain-shrewd, he never came off worse
Exchanging currency, but filled his purse.
So well he managed borrowing and lending,
You'd never guess he had no cash for spending.
He was a man of merit, all the same –
I wish I could recall the fellow's name.

The Scholar

THERE was an Oxford Scholar, a priest in training;
Philosophy, his subject, he found sustaining.
His horse was lean and lanky as a rake,
And he was none too fat, there's no mistake,
But frail and hollow-cheeked and rather sad,
And in a threadbare jacket he was clad.
He was too aloof to seek employment;
In worldly matters he saw no enjoyment.
He would rather have beside his bed
Twenty volumes bound in black and red
Than costly robes or psalter. Even so,
The clue to making gold he did not know.
Any money that his friends might lend,
At once on books and learning he would spend,
Then offer grateful prayers in return
For the souls of those who gave him means to learn.
Knowledge above all things else he heeded,
And never uttered one word more than needed –

Formal, to the point, respectful too,
And shot with lofty thinking through and through.
Full to the brim with goodness was his speech,
And he would gladly learn and gladly teach.

Patient Griselda

THE SCHOLAR'S TALE

I

In the west of Italy at the foot of cold Mount Vesulus there is a rich and fertile plain, with many old castles and towns. It is called Saluzzo. A Duke named Walter ruled it once. Strong and vigorous, courteous and honourable, he took a great delight in hunting and was much liked. But he never thought of the future and – worse still – he would not marry.

This troubled his people and one day a group of them came and tried to persuade him to change his mind.

'Noble lord,' said their spokesman. 'We have a request to make. You are humane, and we know that you will consider it carefully. We have always been happy in your service, but there is one thing that worries us – you have no wife. Whether we sleep or wake, roam or ride, time flies fast and waits for no man. Though your green youth is still in flower, yet age creeps on as quiet as a stone, and we can none of us escape death. Allow us, sir, to choose a wife for you from the ranks of the noblest in the land. And lose no time about it. We should hate it if you died without an heir and our country passed into a stranger's hands.'

'My dear people,' said the Duke, deeply moved, 'so you want to take from me the freedom which I value highly, and freedom is seldom found in marriage. But your advice is full of good sense. I will agree to get married as soon as I can. But you must allow me to choose my own wife. And whoever it is that I choose, you must promise to respect and obey her as long as she lives, as though she were an emperor's daughter. And you must accept my choice without question.'

They agreed to all this and asked him to fix a date for the wedding as soon as possible. This he did, and he started preparations at once.

2

Not far from the Duke's palace was a pleasant village, where poor folk kept their animals and made as good a living from the land as they could.

The poorest of them all was a man named Janicula, and

he had a beautiful young daughter Griselda. As she had been brought up in poverty, she was quite free from sensual desire. She drank water from the well rather than wine from the cask, and was never idle. She was also mature and serious-minded for her age; she looked after her old father devotedly and spun at the wheel while watching her sheep in the field. She brought home roots and herbs, which she cut up and boiled for their meal, then made her bed, which was a hard one.

Walter had often noticed her when he was out hunting. He had been struck by her beauty and goodness and had decided that, if ever he married, she and no other would be his choice.

The wedding morning came and no one knew who the bride would be. There were many who wondered if the Duke meant to marry at all. All the same he had ordered jewellery for Griselda, brooches and rings set in gold and lapis-lazuli, and he had had wedding clothes made to her size. The whole palace was decorated, the kitchens and larders filled with the finest food in Italy.

Then the Duke, magnificently dressed, and his lords and ladies rode out together to Griselda's village. Griselda, who had no idea that all this pomp was for her, had gone to fetch water from the well and was hurrying home. She didn't want to miss the Duke. 'I'll stand with the other girls by our door,' she thought. 'There'll be time for me to get my work done first, then I'll watch the bride as she rides to the castle.'

She was just about to step indoors, when she heard the Duke call her name. She put down her water-pot beside the ox-stall and knelt.

'Where's your father, Griselda?' said the Duke.

'He is here and ready, sir,' she replied. And she went in and brought her father out.

The Duke took the old man by the hand and drew him aside. 'Janicula, I can hide my heart no longer. If you agree, I will marry your daughter and love her all my life. I know you are my faithful servant. Will you have me as your son-in-law?'

The old man blushed and began to tremble. All he could manage to say was, 'Sir, my wish is your wish. You are my dear lord, and in this matter you must do as you please.'

'The three of us must go into your cottage and discuss this together,' said the Duke. 'It shall all be done in your presence. I will say nothing out of your hearing.'

They went into the cottage. Griselda, bewildered to be facing so important a guest in her home, turned very pale.

'Griselda,' he said, 'I would like to marry you, and your father agrees. Are you willing? But as it is all being done so hastily, there are one or two things I must ask you first. Will you always obey me in everything? Whether I make you laugh or cry, will you promise never to grumble or give me sullen looks? Give me your promise, and I will marry you at once.'

'Sir, I do not deserve so much honour,' replied Griselda, amazed and trembling. 'But your wish is my wish. I promise never to disobey you in deed or thought, even if it costs me my life – and I don't want to die.'

'My own Griselda,' said the Duke. He took her to the cottage door and said to the crowd outside, 'This is my wife standing beside me. If you respect and love me, then respect and love her too. That is all I have to say.'

Fine ladies from the court took off her old rags – they didn't much like touching them – and dressed her from top to toe in a splendid new dress. They combed her untidy hair and with their dainty fingers put a crown on her head and adorned her with jewels. She was transformed.

Then the Duke married her with a ring he had brought for the purpose, set her on a fine snow-white horse, and led her in a procession back to the palace. And they spent the day in revelry till the sun went down.

From this day God looked on her with such favour that it

seemed as if she had been brought up in an emperor's hall instead of a hovel. Even people who had known her from birth could hardly believe she was Janicula's daughter. She was gentle and kind, eloquent and discreet, and everyone loved and admired her. People would come from all over the country just to see her.

So Duke Walter was blessed in his marriage. Because he had seen that true goodness can be found in the humblest home, he was respected as a man of wise judgment – and there aren't many of them about. If there were quarrels or grievances, Griselda's tact and good sense soon settled them.

3

Not long after, Griselda had a baby daughter, and there was great rejoicing.

Before the child was weaned, the Duke felt an irresistible desire to test Griselda's constancy. He had often done so before and always found her faultless. What was the point of upsetting her so needlessly again? But he couldn't help himself.

At night he went to her alone and spoke sternly. 'Griselda, you haven't forgotten how I rescued you from poverty, have you? Of course you are very dear to me. But my noblemen resent you. They are ashamed of having to work for someone born in a tiny village, and all the more so since your baby was born. As I want to live in peace with them, I must humour them. I will have to take your baby away. I want to see if you will be as patient and obedient as you promised on our wedding day.'

Griselda's expression did not change as she answered. 'My lord, my baby and I are yours. Do as you wish with us. Time and death will not change my attitude.'

The Duke was pleased with her answer, but pretended not to be. Grimly he left the room. A day or two later he sent to Griselda an officer who seized the baby roughly, as if he meant to kill it.

Griselda did not stir. She sat as meek and quiet as a lamb, then asked if she might kiss the child before it died. Sadly she picked her up, cradled her in her arms, blessed and kissed her, and said, 'Good-bye, my child. I shall never see you again. May Christ, who died on a tree, comfort you.' She handed the baby to the officer. 'I ask only one thing,' she said. 'If you kill the baby, bury her in some place where wild animals and birds can't find her.'

Without a word he took the baby and went away.

He went straight to the Duke and told him Griselda's reaction and exactly what she had said. Though he felt sorry for her, the Duke did not relent. He told the officer to take the baby secretly to Bologna, to his sister the Countess of Panico. The officer was to explain everything to her and ask her to bring up the child in a way that fitted her noble rank. But her origin was to be kept a secret.

The officer did as he was told.

After this the Duke kept a careful watch on Griselda. But her attitude to him did not change at all. She was as cheerful, humble, obedient and affectionate as ever. Nor did she ever once mention her daughter's name.

4

Four years later, Griselda had a son. When he was two years old, Duke Walter decided to test his wife's constancy again. He told her that the people now liked their marriage less than ever. All the grumbles and rumours that he heard upset him greatly. 'I hear them say, "When Walter dies, shall the family of Janicula succeed him and be our master? There's no one else." I can't turn a deaf ear to all this. I want to live in peace if I can. I shall have to treat the boy as I did his sister. But I wanted to tell you first. Please be patient.'

'As I have always said, my only wish is to please you,' replied Griselda. 'If you kill both my daughter and my son, I shall not grieve. They have brought me nothing but illness, sorrow and pain. You are our master; do what you like with us, and don't ask my advice. Just as I took the clothes you gave me and left my own at home when I first came to you, so I gave up my freedom too and bowed to your will. Do as you want, and I will obey. I would gladly die to please you. Death means nothing to me compared with our love.'

Amazed at her constancy and patience, the Duke lowered his eyes. And away he went, with drawn face, but inwardly contented.

The same hateful officer who had so cruelly taken away Griselda's daughter now snatched her beautiful little son. She showed no sign of distress, but kissed her boy and gave him her blessing. She asked the officer to bury the child's fragile body in the earth, safe from birds and wild animals. Quite unmoved, he did not answer, but went on his way and brought the child to Bologna.

The Duke was astonished at her patience. Had he not known already how perfectly she loved her children, he would have thought her malicious or cold. But he knew very well that, after himself, she loved her children best.

What more proof could a husband want of a wife's constancy? But there's no stopping some people when they've set their minds to a certain course. He looked to see if there was any change in her attitude to him. But she never changed; she was always the same. With the years she grew, if anything, even more devoted.

No, it was not Griselda's attitude to Walter but the people's attitude that changed. There were rumours that he had murdered his children, because of their mother's humble origins. Their love for him turned to hatred. Even so, he persisted in his cruel purpose.

When his daughter was twelve years old, he sent a message to the Court of Rome, asking for his marriage to Griselda to be annulled. A papal bull giving him permission to marry again if he wanted was forged and published in full. He hoped that this would heal the trouble between his people and himself. Griselda must have been heartbroken, but she was as humbly determined as ever to stand up to this latest blow of fortune. At the same time the Duke sent a secret letter to Bologna. In it he asked his sister's husband, the Earl of Panico, to bring his two children home, but not to tell anyone whose children they were. He was to say that his daughter was going to marry the Duke of Saluzzo.

The Earl did as he was asked. At daybreak, with a company of noblemen to escort the young girl and her brother, he set out for Saluzzo. The boy was seven years old and dressed in bright new clothes. His sister was wearing her wedding dress, sparkling with jewels. And so they came to Saluzzo.

5

Meanwhile the Duke cruelly decided to test his wife once again. One day in front of all his courtiers he spoke roughly to her.

'You have been true and obedient, Griselda, and a good wife. But a Duke is not as free as a ploughman to do as he likes. My people are crying out to me to take another wife, and the Pope agrees. My new wife is already on her way here. Be brave and go back to your father's house.'

She answered patiently, 'My lord, I know there was no comparison between your magnificence and my poverty. I was never worthy to be your wife. You made me lady of your house, but I have always thought of myself as your humble servant. I will gladly go back to my father and live with him till the end of my life. I'll stay there as your widow and take no other husband. May your new wife bring you happiness.'

'I will allow you to take back with you the dowry you brought me.'

'But I brought nothing except the rags I was wearing, and it would be difficult for me to find them now. How gentle and kind you were to me on our wedding day! It's only too true that love is not the same when it grows old. You will remember how you had me dressed in rich clothes. I brought you nothing but my trust and my poverty. I now return your clothes to you, also my wedding ring. The jewels you gave me are in your room. I must go now.'

'You may keep the smock you are wearing,' said the Duke in a broken voice, so moved that he could hardly speak. And he went out of the room.

There, in front of the people, she stripped herself to her smock, then walked barefoot and bare-headed to her father's house.

The people followed her, weeping and cursing fate for what had happened. But there were no tears in Griselda's eyes, and she said not a word.

Her father soon heard the news. He cursed the day that he was born. He had always had his doubts about the marriage, and expected that the Duke would want to get rid of a wife so far beneath him. When he saw her coming, he hurried out to meet her. While the tears streamed down his cheeks, he tried to cover her with her old coat, but the cloth was too rough and old and it would not properly fit.

So for a time this flower of wifely patience stayed with her father. Neither in word nor look did she show how badly she had been treated, nor did her face give any hint that she remembered her recent high position. People speak of Job's patience, and scholars praise it – especially patience in men. But they don't praise women much. Yet the truth is that no man can be as patient as a woman, nor half as faithful; or if so, then I've never met one who was.

6

In great splendour the Earl of Panico arrived from Bologna, and everyone was talking about the new lady he had brought with him for Duke Walter.

Before their arrival the Duke had sent for Griselda. He told her, as she knelt in front of him, 'I am going to marry this lady and I am determined that she shall receive a royal welcome. As I have no woman here as capable as you are, I am leaving all the arrangements to you, Griselda. It doesn't matter if your clothes are a mess. Just do the best job you can.'

'I am happy to help you, my lord,' she said. And she began to tidy the house, set the tables, make the beds. She got the maids to carry on with their sweeping and shaking, and worked harder herself than any of them.

The Earl arrived about the middle of the morning, and with him were his two children. The people ran out to meet them. When they saw the girl, they said, 'Walter is no fool to want to change his wife. The girl is more beautiful than Griselda, and younger too. Because of her high birth, their children too should be finer. And what a handsome boy her brother is!'

'How fickle and frivolous people are! They change like a weathercock, they wax and wane like the moon, their judgment isn't worth a penny.' That is what the serious-minded in the city thought. But everyone else just stared and gaped, pleased with the novelty of having a new lady in the town.

What about Griselda meanwhile?

She was busy getting things ready for the wedding feast. Quite unworried by her torn and shabby clothes, she went cheerfully to the gate with everyone else to greet the new lady. She received the guests warmly, treating each according to his rank, and praising the young bride with sincerity and feeling. People were amazed that anyone so poorly dressed could be so competent and tactful, and they wondered who she could be.

At last, when everyone was seated at table, the Duke called Griselda to him and said jokingly, 'How do you like my wife, Griselda? Isn't she beautiful?'

'I like her very much, my lord,' she replied. 'I've never seen anyone lovelier. God bless her, and I hope you will both be happy. But one thing I ask you – do not torment her as you have done others. She has been delicately brought up. I don't think she could stand up to suffering as well as someone brought up in adversity.'

Walter was moved by Griselda's words. She was so patient, so free from malice or bitterness, that he said, 'That will do, my own Griselda. Don't distress yourself any more, the evil is ended. I have tested your kindness and constancy to the very limit, and I know how faithful you are.' And he took her in his arms and kissed her.

Griselda was so bewildered she hardly knew what was happening.

'Griselda,' said the Duke, 'by God who died for us, you are my wife. I have no other and never have had. This girl, whom you supposed to be my wife, is my daughter. That boy is my son and heir, and both are your children too. I kept them secretly in Bologna, not in malice or cruelty, not to harm or kill them – God forbid! – but to keep them hidden away till I could be sure of your strength of purpose and faithfulness to me.'

When she heard this, Griselda fainted for joy. On coming round, she called the children to her, then hugged and kissed them as the tears streamed down her cheeks.

'Thank you, God,' she said, 'for keeping my children for me. Oh my dear ones, your mother thought you had been eaten by dogs or worms, but God in His mercy and your kind father kept you safe.'

Again she fainted, still clasping her children so tightly

that it was difficult to release them from her arms. And the crowd were moved to tears.

When she recovered she looked ashamed. But Walter comforted her, and it was a delight to see the reborn happiness between them. The ladies led her to her room, took off her rags and dressed her in cloth of gold, with a crown of rich jewels on her head. Then they brought her into the hall, where everyone did honour to her.

So a sad day ended happily, and there was joy and revelry till the stars came out and the dark sky shone with light.

For many years these two lived prosperously and peacefully. Walter married his daughter to a rich and distinguished Italian lord, and made a home in his court for his wife's old father Janicula for the rest of his life. His son succeeded to the dukedom on his father's death. He too was fortunate in his marriage, but he never put his wife to any demanding test. The world of today is not as harsh as yesterday's.

This story does not mean that wives ought to copy Griselda's patience – they would not succeed, however hard they tried. What it does mean is that everyone should face up to misfortune as steadfastly as Griselda did. I'm afraid that nowadays if you searched a whole city you'd be lucky to find a single Griselda.

The Poet, Geoffrey Chaucer

AFTER the tale it was our Host who spoke;
He frowned at me and began to jest and joke:
'What man are you? Are you hunting for a hare?
For always on the ground I see you stare.
Come over here, lift up that studious chin. . .
Move over, gentlemen, make way for him.
Although he rides so dumbly and sedately,
His waist is trim as mine is, quite as shapely;
And any woman with a pretty face
Would call him poppet, kiss him and embrace.
But he makes our journey tedious, unenriched
By chat or gossip – he must have been bewitched.'

The Sea Captain

THERE was a Sea Captain from the west
Who came from Dartmouth, so I would have guessed.
He rode as best he could on a farmer's horse;
His tunic reached to the knee – the cloth was coarse;
A dagger from a shoulder cord hung down
Under his arm; his skin was tanned and brown.
Quite conscienceless, in France he sneaked on board
Much wine he'd stolen while the merchant snored.
In pirate fights, if he gained the upper hand,
His prisoners walked the plank and swam for land.
From Hull to Carthage there was none to match him
In seamanship; he let no danger catch him;
He knew each current and tide; he'd had to rough
Many a tempest and was shrewd and tough;
Familiar too with all the ports there were
From Gottland to the Cape of Finisterre,
And every creek in Brittany and Spain.
The Captain's boat was called the 'Madelayne'.

A Hundred-Franc Loan

THE SEA CAPTAIN'S TALE

THERE was once a merchant who lived at St Denis. He was shrewd as well as rich. His wife was a great beauty; she had expensive tastes, for she was sociable and enjoyed parties, dancing and fine clothes. For such luxuries, it's always the wretched husband who has to pay. If he can't or won't, then someone else must or it means borrowing, and that's always dangerous.

This merchant had a fine house. His many guests included a handsome young monk, about thirty years old, who was often there. They had both been born in the same village, and the monk, whose name was Brother John, claimed to be his cousin. The merchant was proud of the relationship. The monk was very generous and brought presents for everyone, including the lowliest page. The whole household was as glad to see him as a bird is to greet the rising sun.

One day it happened that the merchant had to go to Bruges on business. He sent a message to Paris inviting Brother John to come and spend a few days with them before he left. Brother John did not need much persuading, and he soon got permission from his Abbot to go to St Denis and inspect some Abbey property in the neighbourhood. As usual he brought with him a cask of Malmsey wine and another of Italian red wine, which they spent a day or two enjoying.

On the third day the merchant got up early and went upstairs into his counting-house to attend to the year's accounts and see how he stood. And there he laid out his books and money bags on the counter, gave orders that he was not to be disturbed, and locked himself in. He stayed there till past nine in the morning.

Brother John had also got up early and was walking up and down in the garden saying his prayers. Suddenly he heard a voice behind him.

'Dear Cousin John,' said the merchant's wife, for it was she, 'why are you up so early? Is something wrong?'

'Niece,' he said, 'five hours' sleep is enough for anyone. But you're looking pale, my dear. Have you had a row with your husband? Whatever is the matter?'

The pretty wife shook her head. 'I daren't tell anybody. Oh, I'm so worried. If only I could go right away – or kill myself.'

'Oh, you mustn't do that,' said the monk. 'Tell me what's worrying you. Perhaps I can help. Whatever it is, I promise I won't tell a soul.'

'And I won't either,' she said, 'not even if I'm torn to pieces or have to go to hell.'

So they both promised, then kissed each other fondly.

'Cousin, I can hardly begin to tell you all I've suffered from my husband. I'm sorry to speak like this about your cousin.'

'Cousin?' said the monk. 'He's no more my cousin than that leaf hanging on the tree! I only call him cousin because I want an excuse to see you. Now tell me what's on your mind.'

'Oh, my dear Brother John, I hate to say it, but he's the worst husband that ever was. He's so mean! As you know, there are six things that women – and that includes me – naturally want of their husbands: they want them to be courageous, wise, rich, generous, considerate to their wives, as well as good lovers. Well, my husband's quite different. By next Sunday I have to pay a hundred francs for some new dresses – he expects me to look smart when I go out with him. Could you possibly lend me the money? He mustn't find out. Oh, please do, Brother John. I should be eternally grateful. I'll pay you back, of course.'

'Most certainly I will, my dear. I quite understand the situation. As soon as your husband has gone to Flanders, I'll bring you the money. Don't breathe a word to anyone about it.' And he held her close, then added, 'It's past nine o'clock. I think you'll be wanting to see about dinner soon, won't you? Good-bye for now.'

'Good-bye,' she said. And off she ran as merry as a magpie and told the cooks to hurry up with the dinner. Then she went upstairs to her husband and knocked loudly on the counting-house door.

'*Qui est là?*' he said.

'It's me, dear. How much longer are you going to be with your accounts, all these books and things? Come downstairs, and give the money bags a rest. Aren't you ashamed to keep Brother John waiting all day for his dinner? Let's hear Mass and then have our meal.'

'Wife,' he answered, 'you know nothing about business.

You have no idea how hard we merchants have to work. Only one in six of us can make a profit. We just have to manage as best we can – or else go on a pilgrimage to dodge our creditors. Misfortune is never far away. Tomorrow I must go to Flanders, but I'll be back as soon as I can. Look after the house and don't be extravagant. You have plenty of clothes and food, and there's silver in your purse.'

He shut the door behind him and came downstairs, where they heard Mass then went in to dinner.

After the meal Brother John took the merchant aside and said, 'So you're off to Bruges tomorrow, cousin? God be with you, and don't eat too much – not in this heat. If there's anything I can do for you while you're away, don't hesitate to ask. . . Oh, – there's just one thing. I'd be grateful if you could lend me a hundred francs for a week or two. I want to buy some cattle. Please keep it a secret. I'll repay you promptly.'

'A hundred francs? Oh, that's nothing, dear Cousin John. My gold is yours, and so is all my stuff. Take what you want. But remember, money is a merchant's plough. Without it he can do nothing. So pay me back when you can.'

The merchant fetched a hundred francs and lent them to the monk on the quiet. Then they drank, chatted and strolled about, till it was time for Brother John to return to his Abbey.

Next morning, with his apprentice as guide, the merchant set out for Flanders. On arriving at Bruges, he attended to his business without wasting any time on frivolities.

The Sunday after the merchant had gone, Brother John returned to St Denis, freshly shaven and with a new tonsure. Everybody in the house, down to the smallest page, was delighted to see him. The merchant's wife welcomed him warmly and entertained him handsomely. He gave her the hundred francs and in the morning rode back to his Abbey or somewhere.

In due course the merchant, having settled his affairs, returned to St Denis, where he and his wife feasted and enjoyed each other's company. He told her that he had had to pay so much for his merchandise that he must now raise a loan; he had agreed to pay back twenty thousand crowns quite soon. So, taking some cash with him, he went to Paris to borrow the rest from his friends. The first he called on was Brother John. It was purely a friendly visit – he had not come on business. Brother John welcomed him heartily. The merchant told him all about the splendid bargains he had made; the only difficulty was that he had to raise a loan before his mind could be at rest.

'Well, I'm very glad you're safely home again,' said Brother John. 'If I were a rich man, you would have your twenty thousand crowns at once. It was so kind of you to lend me money the other day. I returned it to your wife last Sunday, by the way. Please give her my best wishes when you see her.'

The merchant, a shrewd and cautious man, raised the loan, paid the money to the Lombard bankers in Paris and got his bond back. Then home he went, as perky as a parrot. He knew very well that he would make a thousand francs profit on his trip.

His wife met him at the gate, as she always did, and they sat up late that night, rejoicing that he was out of debt. In the morning he started kissing her all over again.

'Now that's enough – really that's enough,' she protested.

After a while the merchant smiled and said, 'I'm rather cross with you, my dear – and do you know why? You've made things awkward between me and Cousin John. You ought to have warned me before I left that he had paid you back my hundred francs. I don't think he liked it much when I talked to him about borrowing money – or so it seemed from the look on his face. I never intended to ask him for a thing. Please be more careful in future. Always tell me if a borrower has returned money to you while I was away. Otherwise I might ask him for what he has already paid back.'

His wife was not in the least put out. 'Well, fancy Brother John behaving like that, damn him! It's quite true that he gave me some money. But that was because you are cousins and both like me to dress well, and because he's enjoyed our hospitality here. It's rather awkward for me. But don't worry – I'll pay you back promptly, a little each day. And if I fall behind a bit, well, remember I'm your wife and charge it up to me – I'll pay you as soon as I can. I promise you, I've spent it all on clothes, just to please you. So don't be angry, but let's laugh and enjoy ourselves. I'll pay you back in kisses, my dear. Turn round – and let's see a smile on your face.'

So the merchant laughed – there was no point in scolding. 'Well, wife, I forgive you,' he said. 'But another time don't be so extravagant. And take more care of things when I'm away.'

The Haberdasher, Carpenter, Weaver, Dyer and Upholsterer

A HABERDASHER and a Carpenter,
A Weaver, Dyer and Upholsterer
Were with us, dressed in livery of their Guild.
The silverwork that trimmed their knives was skilled
And matched their purses. Each was worth a place
As alderman or in Guildhall on a dais –
Positions which their wives were quick to claim
For them, as they enjoyed reflected fame.

The Cook

A COOK had travelled with them from the start;
The spice he boiled his chickens with was tart
And mixed with marrowbones and galingale.
Well he knew the taste of London ale
And how to roast and seethe and broil and fry,
Or make a pot of soup and bake a pie.
For chicken puddings, few could vie with him. . .
A shame he had an ulcer on his shin.

The Judge

THERE was a cautious Judge, a man of law,
Discreet, distinguished, and much held in awe,
Or so he seemed, his judgments were so wise.
He often had been Justice in Assize,
And for his skill and lofty reputation
Was paid in fees and robes to suit his station.
Most busy he looked, yet was not so, because
He always seemed much busier than he was.
He could remember every single case
And judgment given since King William's days;
Besides, a deed he could compose and draw
So well that none could find the slightest flaw.
He knew every statute off by rote,
And wore a simple many-coloured coat.

The Wild Waves

THE JUDGE'S TALE

I

IN Syria there was once a company of wealthy merchants, honest and respectable men who sent their spices, satins and cloth of gold all over the world. Some of them stayed in Rome, on business or pleasure, for a month or two at a time. There the name of the Roman Emperor's daughter, Lady Constance, was on everybody's lips. 'There has been no one as good or as beautiful since the world began,' people said. 'Supremely courteous, young, modest and generous, she ought to be queen of all Europe.'

The merchants finished loading their ships then sailed back to Syria, where the Sultan, eager for news, entertained them. Of course they told him about Constance. They spoke so warmly of her that he fell hopelessly in love with her. He sent for his advisers and told them he would die if he could not marry her, and they must find a way to help him.

The advisers argued and made a number of suggestions;
they spoke of charms and of magic, but in the end the only
solution they could see was marriage. Yet there were
difficulties here. Christian and Muhammadan customs
were very different. 'No Christian prince,' they said,
'would allow his child to marry under the law of Muhammad, our prophet.'

'Then I will be baptized a Christian,' said the Sultan.
'Please stop arguing. I insist on marrying Constance.
Marriage to her is the only possible solution. You must get
her for me.'

There's no need to waste time on details. Enough to say
that, with the Pope's mediation, the marriage was agreed,
on condition that the Sultan and all his court became
Christians. They also had to pay a sum of money – I don't
know how much.

The day arrived for Constance's departure. She was to
sail to Syria to marry a man she knew nothing about. No
wonder that her cheeks were pale, and there were tears in
her eyes as she said good-bye to her father and mother.
'You brought me up so lovingly. Except for God above,
you are my greatest joy. Now I must go to Syria, a bar-
barous land, and I shall never see you again. But that is
your wish. Women are at the mercy of men – they have no
power of their own – and are born to suffering. God give
me strength!'

Sadly and solemnly this beautiful and unhappy girl was
brought to the ship. 'God bless you,' she said. They were so
overcome that all they could say was, 'Good-bye, dear
Constance,' nothing more. And away she sailed.

Now the Sultan's mother, an evil woman, was furiously
angry at what had happened. It maddened her to think
that her son was determined to abandon their ancient
faith and marry a Christian. She called her advisers and
said, 'My lords, you know my son's intentions. He is
disobeying the holy laws of the Koran. I would rather die

before Muhammad's law is torn from my heart. This new faith would drag us down to hell. But, my lords, I have a plan which will save us. Will you agree to it?' And when they had promised to live and die with her, she told them her plan. 'First we must pretend to become Christians – cold water can't hurt us much! Then I will provide such a banquet as will give the Sultan what he deserves. His wife, christened white, will need more than a font-ful of water to wash away all the blood.'

A day or two later that vilest of women rode over to the Sultan and promised to be baptized a Christian. She asked for the honour of giving him a banquet on his wedding day, to which the Christians would be invited. The delighted Sultan readily agreed. Then she kissed him and rode back home.

2

The Christians landed in Syria with a magnificent company. At once the Sultan sent a message, first to his mother and then to all the kingdom, to say his wife had arrived. He asked if his mother would do his bride the honour of riding to meet her.

The meeting between the Syrians and the Romans was truly magnificent. The Sultan's mother, splendidly dressed, received Constance like a mother greeting her dearly loved daughter, and they rode off to the city side by side. Julius Caesar's triumphal return to Rome was not more spectacular. But behind all her flattery, that scorpion of a woman, the Sultan's mother, was preparing her deadly sting.

The Sultan came to meet them and welcomed his wife with the greatest delight. But my concern is with what happened a day or two later, at the banquet. This was princely, but the guests paid dearly for it before they rose from table. The Sultan and all the Christians and Syrian converts were stabbed and hacked to pieces at the table. That cruel old crone, the Sultan's mother, had seen to this – she wanted to control the country herself. Constance was carried hot-foot to the harbour and put in a rudderless boat. They gave her some of the treasure she had brought with her, some clothes and plenty of food. Then they pushed the boat out into the salt sea and shouted, 'Now you can teach yourself how to sail back to Italy.'

And Constance, putting her trust in God, the King of heaven, sailed away.

For years and days she floated over the Grecian seas, eating little, expecting death from the wild waves at any moment.

You may wonder why she was not killed at the banquet with the others. My answer is another question: who was it that saved Daniel from the lions? Why didn't she drown at sea? My answer is: who kept Jonah safe inside the whale, till he was spouted up at Nineveh? Who gave this woman food and drink for three years and more? It was Christ, who fed five thousand people with five loaves and two fishes.

She was driven into the wild seas of our ocean, till at last, far away in Northumberland, a wave cast her ashore near a castle whose name I don't know. The boat stuck in the sand so firmly that the tide couldn't shift it.

The Constable of the castle went down to see the wreck. He found an exhausted woman and some treasure that she had brought with her. Speaking a kind of corrupt Latin that he was able to understand, she begged him to kill her, to put her out of her misery. The Constable took her to the castle, but she refused to reveal who she was. She said that the sea had so confused her that she had lost her memory. The Constable and his wife Hermengyld took pity on her and let her stay with them. Of course, like nearly everyone else in the country, they were pagans. But Constance was so kind, so anxious to please, that everybody loved her. In time Hermengyld became a Christian.

Yet cruel fate was still hard on Constance's track. A young knight fell violently in love with her, but she rejected all his advances. This made him so angry that he thought up a scheme to make her die a shameful death. One night, when the Constable was away, he crept into Hermengyld's bedroom while she was asleep, with Constance lying beside her. He stole up to the bed, cut Hermengyld's throat, laid the blood-stained knife beside Constance, and crept away.

Soon afterwards the Constable returned, bringing with him his friend Alla, King of Northumberland. Alla had been King for several years and was famous for his victories against the Scots. When the Constable found his wife so cruelly murdered, he was overcome with grief. And when he saw the knife at Constance's side, he could not believe his eyes. He asked her what had happened, but she was too distraught to answer. He ran to King Alla and brought him into the bedroom. Everyone in the castle followed him and crowded round the door.

Now King Alla had already heard Constance's story from the Constable. Far from being angry or suspicious, he was filled with pity for her. It hurt him to see so kind and gentle a creature in such acute distress. Nobody believed that Constance, who had lived so virtuously and was so fond of Hermengyld, could be guilty of so monstrous a crime – nobody except the young knight who had killed Hermengyld. This made the King suspicious, and he decided to look more deeply into the case.

Constance, who felt she had no one to champion her and could not defend herself, knelt down and prayed, 'Father in heaven, if I am innocent, oh save me from death.' Pale and lonely, an Emperor's daughter far from home, she looked up and caught King Alla's eye. Tears were running down his cheeks, and his face was full of compassion.

'Someone fetch a holy book,' he said. 'If the knight will swear upon it that Constance murdered this woman, we will consider our sentence.'

A British gospel was brought, and on this the knight swore that she was guilty.

Next moment a hand struck him on the neck-bone. He fell like a stone and lay on the floor.

Then a voice from heaven rang out, 'In the King's presence you have slandered an innocent daughter of the Church. How can I stay silent?'

Everyone, except the innocent Constance, was terrified. As for the knight, Alla had him put to death for perjury.

As a result of the miracle the King, and many others who had witnessed it, were converted to the Christian faith. Soon afterwards King Alla married Constance, and she became his Queen.

The only person who objected to the marriage was Donegild, the King's tyrannical old mother. She hated the idea of his marrying this foreign woman. She thought her heart would burst in two.

Some time after the wedding Alla, leaving his wife in the care of the Constable and a bishop, went to Scotland to fight his enemies. He was still away when she gave birth to a son, whom she called Maurice. The Constable wrote to Alla to give him the happy news and sent a messenger with the letter. But the messenger, expecting to gain advantage for himself, went first to the King's mother and told her of the birth. 'Madam,' he said, 'the Constable has sent me to the King with this letter to give him the news. If you would like to send him anything, I shall be pleased to take it.'

'Not just yet,' said Donegild. 'But if you will stay the night here, I'll have a letter ready for you in the morning.'

She saw to it that he had plenty of ale and wine to drink. While he was asleep and snoring like a pig, she stole the letter from his box. Then she replaced it with one that she had written herself to the King, forging the Constable's signature. Her letter said that the Queen's baby son was a monstrous creature, so horrible that no one dared to stay in the castle. The mother was a loathsome witch.

When he read the letter, the King was greatly distressed. He spoke to nobody of his sorrow, but wrote back in his own hand, 'I accept what God has sent. Look after the child, whether ugly or beautiful, and my wife too, till I come home. Christ in his good time may send me an heir more to my liking.' Hiding his tears, he sealed the letter, then gave it to the messenger to take home.

On his return journey the messenger again stopped for the night at Donegild's court. Once again he drank himself silly, then fell asleep and snored the night away till sunrise. Once again the Queen-mother stole the letter. She replaced it with another one which read, 'The King orders his Constable, on pain of death, to forbid Constance to remain in his kingdom for more than three days longer. He must put her, the young child, and all her things in the same boat as he found her, push it out to sea, and tell her never to return.'

Next morning when he woke, the messenger took the shortest way to the castle and gave the letter to the Constable, who read it at once. 'How can this wicked world, so full of sin, survive?' he exclaimed bitterly. 'The innocent suffer, the wicked prosper – oh, why does a righteous God allow it? Dear Constance, I must either be your executioner or die a shameful death. I have no other choice.'

On the fourth day Constance, pale as death, with her baby in her arms, walked down to the boat. Resigned as ever to God's will, she knelt down on the crowded shore and said, 'He that saved me in the castle from an unjust accusation will protect me now in the salt sea. I cannot see how He will do it. But He is my rudder and my sail, and I trust Him.'

Her little child lay weeping in her arms. Still kneeling, 'Peace, little son,' she said tenderly. 'I won't hurt you.' She took the scarf from her head and laid it over his eyes to shield them from the sun. Then she rocked him in her arms to hush his crying. Looking up to heaven, 'Mary, mother of God,' she said, 'I know my suffering cannot compare with yours. You saw your son killed in front of you, but mine is still alive. Have pity on him.'

The Constable, who had been getting the boat ready, was now walking towards her.

'Dear Constable,' she begged, 'let my child stay with you.' Though she saw the anguish on the Constable's face, the conflict between duty to his King and the promptings of his heart, she knew already that he must obey the King. 'If you daren't save him, then kiss him once in his father's name.'

And with this she had to be content. As the Constable, with tears in his eyes, kissed the boy, she felt that it was not he but her ruthless husband who was to blame.

She walked towards the boat, still hushing her baby, while the crowd followed. She said good-bye to them and stepped on board. Thanks to the Constable there was plenty of food there, and everything else she needed. And away she sailed.

God send her fair winds, fine weather, and keep her safe!

3

Soon afterwards King Alla came home to the castle. He asked for his wife and child. The Constable's heart turned cold. He told the King plainly what had happened, just as you have heard, and showed him the letter and the royal seal. 'Sir, I have done what you ordered me to do, on pain of death,' he said.

They fetched the messenger and tortured him till he revealed exactly where he had spent each night of his journey. By careful questioning – though I don't know all the details – they were soon able to guess who wrote the letter and was responsible for the mischief. As a result Alla killed his mother for her treachery. So that was the end of Donegild, and a good thing too. But I cannot begin to tell you how deeply Alla grieved for his wife and child.

For five years and more, in misery and pain Constance braved the wild waves. One stormy day the sea cast her

ashore at the foot of a pagan castle, whose name I don't know. People streamed out of the gates just to stare at her. As darkness fell, the castle steward, while the child screamed, climbed into the boat and tried to grab her. When Constance struggled to throw him off, he tripped and fell over the side and was swept away. Away too went her boat, for ever driving on, now west, now north or south, now east, for many a weary day. Would her sufferings never end?

One day, on the wide and restless sea she saw a ship. It was a Roman ship, far bigger than her own little boat. As she drifted alongside, she looked up at the deck and saw the friendly faces of senators and soldiers looking down at her. The commander was the chief Senator. When he saw the little boat was water-logged and sinking, with a woman and child on board, he had them picked up and brought into the cabin. He told Constance that he was returning to Rome from a victorious expedition against the Syrians. The Emperor had heard some time ago of the massacre of Christians at the feast and of the dishonour done to his daughter by the Sultan's wicked mother, and he had sent an army to take vengeance. The chief Senator had no idea who Constance was or why she came to be in such a plight, and she had no intention of telling him.

He took her to Rome and gave her and her young son to his wife to look after. So they both lived in the Senator's house. His wife was in fact Constance's aunt, but she did not recognize her niece, who had changed so much.

Meanwhile King Alla had begun to feel so much remorse for having killed his mother that he decided to go to Rome to do penance and receive absolution from the Pope. Informed in advance of his arrival, the Senator and some of his family rode out to meet him and gave him a magnificent welcome. King Alla returned the compliment by inviting the Senator to a feast a few days later, and Constance's little son went with him. Some say he went at his mother's request. I'm not certain if that was the reason, but at any rate he was there. While they were eating, he stood beside the King and looked up into his face.

'Who is this pretty child?' the King asked.

'I've no idea,' said the Senator. 'He has a mother, but no father, I believe.' And he told Alla how the child had been found. 'I've never in my life seen or heard of such a saintly woman.'

Alla remembered Constance's face very well, and this child's face was exactly like it. Could she be the boy's mother? 'My head is full of ghosts,' he thought. 'My wife must have drowned long ago. One could hardly expect anything else.' But the next moment he was arguing, 'God brought her before to my own country. Perhaps he has brought her safely here as well.'

In the afternoon, on the off-chance that this might be so, Alla went home with the Senator. Greatly honoured, the Senator sent at once for Constance. When she knew why she had been sent for, she nearly fainted.

The moment he saw her, he knew it really was Constance. He was quite overcome.

But Constance could not forget his unkindness to her. She stood before him as still as a tree, dumb with sadness.

Twice she fainted. With tears in his eyes he told her, 'I swear before God that I am no more the cause of your suffering than Maurice my son. Oh, my dear, how like you he looks.'

The more they wept, the sadder they felt, and it was a long time before their hearts were at ease. What a painful scene it was! But I'll say no more about it now. It would take me all day and night to tell you everything. Finally, when all the truth was known, they must have kissed a hundred times.

Then Constance asked her husband to invite her father the Emperor to dinner one day soon, but to say not a word to him about herself. Some say that the child Maurice took the message. But I prefer to think that Alla did the Emperor the honour of going himself.

The Emperor courteously agreed to come, and Alla returned to his lodging to make the arrangements.

The morning came. King Alla and his wife rode out to meet the Emperor. When she saw him, she dismounted in the street and fell at his feet and said, 'Father, can you remember your daughter Constance? I am she. Long ago you sent me over the salt sea to Syria, alone and doomed to die. Be merciful, dear father. Don't send me again to heathen lands, but thank my husband here for his kindness.'

I'll say no more of this joyful reunion, for it's high time for me to end my story.

In due course Maurice became Emperor and was crowned by the Pope and lived a noble Christian life. But you can read all about him in the history books. My story is about Constance and what happened to her.

King Alla chose a day to take her and the boy by the shortest way back to England. Here they lived in peace and happiness. But earthly happiness never lasts long. It turns from day to night, it changes like the tide. After no more than a year King Alla died, and Constance and the boy returned to Rome, to live there with her father till he too died.

And that really is the end of my story.

The Franklin

THE Judge's friend was a Franklin, it appeared,
Whose face was ruddy and daisy-white his beard.
He loved to dip his bread in wine, when drinking.
Perfect happiness, to his way of thinking,
Lay in sensual pleasures. He was most
Hospitable as householder and host;
His bread and ale were both extremely fine,
His cellars stocked with barrels of best wine,
His larders too with many a tasty pie
Of fish or meat, and in such rich supply
His household seemed to snow with food and drink
And every luxury a man could think.
His coops were filled with partridges; he was fond
Of pike and bream, the fish that filled his pond.
His cook was soon in trouble if he dared
To serve the sauce unspiced, or were unprepared.
A table in the hall would always stay
Laden with food for visitors all day.

At meetings of J.P.s he took the chair;
When Parliament was in session, he was there.
A dagger and a wallet made of silk
Hung at his girdle, white as morning milk.
He'd been a sheriff, was skilled at auditing,
A most distinguished vassal of his king.

The Black Rocks of Brittany

THE FRANKLIN'S TALE

In Brittany there was once a Knight called Arviragus. He loved a lady and did everything in his power to win her. She was the most beautiful lady under the sun and came of so noble a family that he didn't dare to tell her how much he loved her. But she was aware of his feelings. After a while she took pity on him and agreed to have him as her lord and master – as far as a husband can ever be called the master of his wife. He in his turn promised never to be jealous, or to force her to do anything against her will; but, for the sake of appearances, he would be called the master.

Dorigen (for that was her name) thanked the Knight and said, 'Sir, as you have been so generous to me, I promise all my life to be a true and humble wife.' If there's one thing you can be sure of, it's this – if love is to last, it cannot be forced. Once try to force it and the god of love claps his wings and – good-bye to him, he's off! So the agreement between them was a sensible one, and he took her home to his own country, not far from Penmarch, where they settled down contentedly together.

After a year or so Arviragus decided to go to England – also called not Brittany, but Britain – to seek honour and glory in deeds of arms. He was away for two years. Dorigen, who loved him with all her heart, was very distressed by his absence. She wept, she pined for him, as good wives always do when their husbands are away. She couldn't eat or sleep; she lay awake lamenting. Her heart so ached for him that the world meant nothing to her, and in spite of the patient efforts of her friends – day and night they told her she was killing herself for nothing – she would not be comforted. Letters from Arviragus, saying he was well and would soon be back home, arrived just in time to save her from dying of a broken heart. Her friends begged her on their knees for heaven's sake to go out walking with them and drive away her melancholy thoughts. And at long last she agreed.

Now her castle stood near the sea, and she often liked to walk with her friends along the cliff top and watch the ships sailing by. But when she saw them, her sorrow came surging back, and she would cry, 'Is there no ship among all these to bring my husband home and ease the pain in my heart?' And her eyes would fill with tears. At other times she would sit and think and gaze sadly down at the sea and say, 'Eternal God, whose wisdom guides the world, didst Thou create these fiendish and grisly black rocks? They are no use to man, bird or beast. Their only work is to destroy. A hundred thousand men – men whom Thou madest in Thine own image – have perished here. Dear God, who made the wind to blow, keep my husband safe! These rocks kill my heart with fear. I wish they were sunk into hell.' And she would weep bitterly. Then her friends, noticing that the sea only made her grief worse, led her inland to springs and rivers and other places of delight, where they danced and played chess and backgammon.

One morning early in May, they went to a garden nearby to picnic and amuse themselves for the day. Gentle showers had painted every leaf and flower, bringing out their scents and colours. It was a paradise of beauty and delight, enough to rejoice any heart that ever was born, unless great sickness or sorrow prevented it. After dinner they danced and sang, except for Dorigen, who sat by herself, wishing that her husband were there to dance with her. Ah well, she must endure for a while longer and go on hoping.

Among the dancers was a young Squire called Aurelius. He was brighter and more finely dressed than the month of May itself. No one since the world began had ever sung and danced as well as he. He was strong, handsome, rich, wise, capable, popular – everyone thought the world of him. But unfortunately, quite unknown to Dorigen, he had fallen in love with her. He had not dared to tell her, but for two years had said not a word; he had drunk his cup of suffering to the dregs. Only the songs, lyrics and ballads he composed gave any hint of his feelings; and though he sang them in her presence, she never guessed their true meaning.

Well, it happened on this beautiful May morning that before they left the garden he got talking with her. Seizing his chance, he went straight to the point and told her of his love.

'Madam,' he said, 'I wish to God I had gone to England with Arviragus and never returned. I know that my devotion to you is in vain, and all I shall get from it is a broken heart. Have pity on my dreadful suffering. One word from you can kill me or save me. Oh, I wish I could die here now and be buried at your feet!'

Dorigen was astounded. 'Do you really mean this?' she said. 'I had no idea. Now I know how you feel. But, by God who gave me life, I swear I will never in word or deed be an unfaithful wife. I shall stay with the man I'm married to. That is my final answer.' And she added jokingly, 'Heavens above, Aurelius, since you are so upset, I'll agree to be your love on one condition. You must first remove all these rocks, stone by stone, from one end of Brittany to the other, so that they are no longer a danger to shipping. Clear the coast completely, till not a single stone is left, and I'll promise to love you better than any other man.'

'Is this all the mercy you can show me?' he said.

'Yes, by the Lord that made me! For I know very well that it will never happen. So forget your foolishness.'

'Madam, that's quite impossible,' said Aurelius. 'Now I must die a sudden, horrible death.' And away he went.

Soon Dorigen's friends rejoined her, and they wandered up and down the garden till dark – or, as a poet might put it, 'till the horizon had robbed the sun of all its light.' Then they went happily home.

But Aurelius was far from happy. Back in his house, he fell on his knees in despair and, raising his hands to high heaven, began to pray to the gods, especially to Apollo the sun god:

'Lord Apollo, god of every plant and herb and tree and flower, have mercy on wretched Aurelius. I'll tell you how you can help me. Ask your radiant sister Lucina, queen of the sea and of all rivers, to do a miracle. You know how she loves to be lit and kindled at your fire, and how she obeys your will as the tides obey her. Ask her at the next full moon to send a flood, a tide so high that it will submerge the highest rock in Brittany five fathoms deep. Let the moon stay at full and the high tide continue day and night for two years. Then I can say to my lady, "Keep your promise. The rocks have gone." '

He fell down in a swoon and lay for a long time in a trance. At last his brother, who knew of his misery, came in and carried him off to bed.

Soon after this Arviragus came home, full of honour and glory. At last Dorigen could clasp in her arms the distinguished soldier who loved her as much as life itself. His one thought was to dance and joust and make her happy.

Aurelius took no part in this. For two years he lay ill in bed, in great distress. All this time he had only his brother to comfort him – a scholar, to whom alone he told all his troubles. At last the brother remembered a book of magic which he had once seen in Orleans during his student days. A friend of his, a bachelor of law, had hidden it in his desk. There was a lot in the book about the working of the twenty-eight mansions of the moon, and other nonsense that no one believes nowadays, for Holy Church keeps us clear of that sort of thing. At the thought of this book his heart danced for joy, and he said to himself: 'I'm sure a magician could conjure up all kinds of wonderful sights – perhaps a lion, or a vine with red and white grapes, or flowers in a field, or a barge rowing up and down – and they would vanish whenever he pleased, for none of them would be real. Why shouldn't he for a week or two make it look as if the black rocks of Brittany had vanished, and ships could come and go along the coast? Then my brother would be cured, and the lady would have to keep her promise or be disgraced for ever.'

Well, to cut the story short, Aurelius and his brother set off at once for Orleans. Just outside the town they met a young scholar, who greeted them in Latin and said, 'I know why you've come here.' Then he told them exactly what they had decided to do. Only a magician could have managed that.

Aurelius dismounted from his horse, and the magician took them to his house and put them at their ease. Before supper he showed them some amazing sights – parks full of wild deer, hawks killing a heron, knights jousting on a plain, and finally Dorigen herself dancing – and her partner seemed to be Aurelius! Then the magician clapped his hands, and the whole entertainment vanished. There were just the three of them there, sitting in the study among his books, and they had seen all these marvels without ever stirring from the house.

After supper they discussed how much the magician should be paid for removing all the rocks of Brittany from Gironde to the mouth of the Seine. He made some difficulties and swore, God help him, that he wouldn't take less than a thousand pounds.

'What's a thousand pounds?' said Aurelius gaily. 'If I were master of it, I'd give the whole wide world – which people say is round. It's a bargain, then. You'll be paid in full, I promise.'

Aurelius slept soundly that night. In the morning at daybreak he and the magician went straight back to Brittany.

It was the cold and frosty season of December. Bitter frosts, with sleet and rain, had destroyed the green in every garden. The sun was old and thinly shining – the colour of pale copper, no longer the burnished gold of full summer.

Encouraged by Aurelius, the magician started at once on his experiments – or, shall I say, his conjuring tricks? I'm afraid I know nothing whatever about tables of roots, centres and angles, proportionals, and all the rest of his astrological mish-mash. But at last everything was ready; the right moment had arrived, and he delayed no longer. So powerful was the spell the magician made that, whisht! all the rocks seemed to vanish, not one of them was left.

Night and day Aurelius had waited in anguish for this miracle. He fell to his knees and thanked the magician. Then off he went to look for Dorigen.

He found her in the temple and greeted her with trembling heart. 'My own true lady,' he said, 'I love and honour you with all my heart. Now I must speak out or die. You are torturing me to death – please be merciful. Do you remember your promise to me in the garden? Unworthy as I am, you swore to love me best. Now my life is in your hands. I've done what you commanded – all the rocks of Brittany have vanished. Go and see for yourself.' And he left her.

She went to the cliff top and saw no rocks in the sea. Dorigen had never expected to fall into such a trap. She was aghast. The colour drained from her cheeks. 'Oh, how can this have happened?' she cried. 'This monstrous miracle – I never dreamed it possible. It's against the laws of nature.'

Home she went, so distressed and frightened she could hardly walk. For a day or two she wept, lamented, fainted, even thought of killing herself rather than be unfaithful to her husband.

Arviragus came home and found her in tears. When he asked her why she was weeping, the tears fell all the faster.

'Oh, I wish I'd never been born!' she cried. 'I said – I promised –' And she told him all that I've been telling you. There's no need for me to say it all over again.

Her husband remained calm and unruffled. 'Is there anything else, Dorigen?' he said, affectionately.

'No, no,' she said. 'Isn't this more than enough?'

'Wife,' he answered, 'let sleeping dogs lie. All may yet be well. But you must accept your situation and keep your word. There's nothing more sacred than a promise.' Then he burst into tears and cried out, 'I forbid you to breathe a word of this to anyone. I'll bear my sorrow as best I can – but don't look sad, or people will suspect there's something wrong.'

Then he called a squire and maidservant to him. 'Go with Dorigen,' he told them, 'and take her wherever she tells you.'

Dorigen knew now where she must go, and off she went to the town with her two puzzled attendants. In the middle of a crowded street she met Aurelius. Their meeting was no accident, for he kept a watch on her movements, had seen her leave the house and was following her. He greeted her happily and asked where she was going.

'To the garden to keep my promise, as my husband bade me,' she answered distractedly.

Aurelius began to wonder. He felt so sorry for her, as well as for Arviragus. The chivalrous Knight would rather lose his greatest delight than see her break her promise. Such generosity and nobility of mind were infectious. Aurelius felt mean to be behaving as he was.

'Madam,' he said, 'your distress and your husband's goodness touch my heart. Tell him that I would rather suffer agony for ever than destroy the love between you both. I release you from every promise you have made to me. I shall never reproach you for anything. And now I say good-bye to the best and truest lady I have ever known.'

So a squire, you see, can be as noble as a knight. And women? They should think twice before making promises – or at least remember Dorigen.

She knelt and thanked Aurelius, then went home to her husband. You can imagine how overjoyed he was. He and Dorigen lived together supremely happy for the rest of their lives. Never did an angry word pass between them, and she was true to him for ever.

That's enough now about those two. What of Aurelius?

Having lost everything, he cursed the day he was born. 'Oh, I wish I'd never promised that magician a thousand pounds in gold. What am I to do? I'm ruined. I'll have to sell my inheritance and go begging in the streets. I can't stay here and bring disgrace on all my family. I wonder if he'd let me pay off my debt, a little at a time. I'll go and ask him. Whatever happens, I'll keep my promise.'

Gloomily he went to his treasure chest and took out some five hundred pounds in gold, which he gave to the magician, begging him to be generous and give him time to pay the rest. 'Master, I've never yet failed to keep a promise. I'll pay my debt to you, even though I have to go begging, with nothing but a shirt to my back. But if you could give me – on security – two or three years in which to pay, then I could manage it. Otherwise I'd have to sell my inheritance.'

'Haven't I kept my bargain with you?' said the magician.

'Yes, indeed you have.'

'And haven't you enjoyed your lady's love?'

'No, no,' he answered mournfully.

'Why not?'

Then Aurelius told him the whole story – of the Knight's nobility, of Dorigen's distress and how she would rather have died than be unfaithful to him – but I won't weary you by going through it all again. 'She made her promise in all innocence. She'd never heard of magical illusion. I felt so sorry for her that I was as generous to her as her husband was to me – I sent her back to him.'

'Dear brother,' said the magician, 'you all behaved nobly to each other. Well, you're a squire and he's a knight; I'd like to think a magician can behave as nobly too. Sir, I release you from your thousand pounds. All shall be the same as if we'd never met. I won't take a penny from you for my skill or my labour. You've paid for my board, and that's enough. Good-bye.'

He handed back the five hundred pounds, mounted his horse and rode away.

And that's the end of my story. . .

But just a moment! I'd like to ask you a question. Which of them – the Knight, the squire or the magician – seems to you the most generous? Tell me, someone, before we ride any further.

The Doctor

THERE was a Doctor with us. In medicine
And surgery no one compared with him,
And in astronomy he had been well grounded;
His skill with charms and talismans astounded.
There was no disease he could not spot;
He knew the cause, the remedy he'd got
And gave it to the patient there and then,
For he had his chemists standing by, and when
He needed drugs and syrups, they were to hand.
Each lined the other's pockets, you understand;
This profitable friendship was not new.
He'd read the medical textbooks through and through.
He did not overeat, but was interested
Only in dishes easily digested.
No time for Bible study could he find.
His clothes were blood-red and grey-blue, silk-lined.
A careful spender, money he never burned;
In time of plague he put by what he earned.
As gold in medicine makes the patient fit,
He was therefore most attached to it.

The Wife of Bath

THERE was a jolly Wife; from Bath she came,
And she was a little deaf, which seemed a shame.
No weaver was there, even in Ypres or Ghent,
Could weave like her – at the loom her time was spent.
Her kerchiefs of the finest cloth were made;
I daresay that at least ten pounds they weighed,
The ones she wore on Sunday on her head.
Her stockings were a handsome scarlet red
And tightly fastened; her shoes were soft and new.
Her face was comely, bold, of rosy hue;
She was a worthy woman all her life.
Five times in church had she been made a wife,
Apart from other loves she'd known before,
Of whom for the present I need say no more.
Three times to Jerusalem she'd been,
Crossing many a distant foreign stream.
She'd been to papal Rome and to Boulogne,

To holy shrines in Galicia and Cologne;
Fond of the road, she'd travelled much of late.
Her front teeth stood apart, like an open gate.
Comfortably on an ambling horse she sat,
With a graceful wimple, and on her head a hat
As broad as a shield or buckler, round in shape,
With a skirt that did her ample buttocks drape,
And a pair of pointed spurs upon her feet.
How she chattered and laughed along the street!
She knew all the cures for love, for it must be said
That was a theme she'd learnt from A to Z.

The Queen's Riddle

THE WIFE OF BATH'S TALE

LONG ago, in the days of King Arthur, the whole country was enchanted. The Fairy Queen and her merry company often danced in the fields. At least, that's what people used to believe, so I've read. But today there are no more fairies left. Holy friars, with their overpowering Christian kindness, have driven them all away. These friars haunt the place, thick as motes in a sunbeam. They go about blessing halls, bedrooms, kitchens, cities and villages, castles and cowsheds – no wonder the fairies have vanished. Wherever a fairy used to be, you find a friar muttering his prayers.

Now King Arthur had in his court a lively young knight. One day, as the Knight came riding from the river, he saw a young lady out walking and seduced her. There was such an uproar that he was condemned to death and would have been executed, had not the Queen and her ladies pleaded with the King for his life. So the King handed him over to the Queen and, much to her delight, left it to her to decide what was to be done about him.

As soon as she had a chance to speak to the Knight, she said to him, 'Sir, you realize that your life is now in my hands. I'll pardon you on one condition – you must answer the question: what is it that women most desire? You'd better be careful, if you want to keep your neck-bone from the steel. If you can't give me the answer now, I'll give you a year and a day to find it. But first I must have your word that you won't run away. You must surrender yourself to this court when your time is up.'

The Knight sighed gloomily – he was most upset. But

what else could he do but agree? So he decided to come back at the end of a year with whatever answer God might provide him. Then he gave his word to the Queen and took his leave.

Up and down the country from house to house he went, questioning everybody he met. But nowhere could he find two people to agree on the answer. Some said that women love riches best; others said position, a life of pleasure, splendid clothes, or often getting widowed and remarried. Some thought that the way to women's hearts is through flattery, and I must admit they're not far wrong about that. Don't we all like to be made a fuss of? Some said we like to have our own way, that we can't stand being criticized or called stupid. That's natural. Even an animal kicks out when scratched on a sore spot. The fact is that no woman can stand too much of the truth about herself. However bad we are, we like to be thought wise and virtuous, reliable – and (some would say) discreet as well. Discreet? That's nonsense. No woman can ever keep a secret.

At last the year was up, and still the Knight had not found his answer. Sadly he turned back for home.

Suddenly, as he was riding past the edge of a wood, he saw some ladies dancing, twenty-four of them, and more. Was there a chance that they might know the answer? He pressed on towards them. But as he drew near, in the flicker of an eyelid they vanished. All he could see in front of him was an ugly old woman. She was sitting on the grass, the ugliest woman he had ever seen.

Sick at heart, the Knight turned his horse towards the wood. But the old woman stood up in front of him and barred the way.

'Sir Knight, there's no road through here,' she said. 'You look worried, sir. What is it you want?'

'An answer to a question,' said the Knight.

'Then ask me. There's not much that old people like myself don't know.'

'I want to know what it is that women most desire. I must bring the answer to the Queen, and failure means death. I'd pay you well for the answer.'

'I'll give it to you gladly,' said the old woman. 'Your payment will be a promise to do the first thing I require of you, if it lies in your power.'

The Knight made his promise.

'Now your life is safe,' said the old woman. 'I'm sure that the Queen will agree that my answer is the right one.' And she whispered it into his ear. 'Now let's ride on together, and waste no more time in talking.'

When they came to Arthur's court, all the ladies assembled to hear the Knight's answer, with the Queen herself as presiding judge. After the question had been put, he did not stand there like a dumb ox, but spoke out in a manly voice for all the court to hear: 'Royal lady, the thing that a woman most desires is to have power over her husband and to be his master. Do what you like with me now. My life is in your hands.'

There was silence in the hall. Not a lady present could contradict him, for all agreed that he had given the right answer.

Up sprang the old woman. 'Mercy, royal lady!' she cried. 'Before you dismiss this court, you must see that I too have justice done to me. It was I that told the Knight his answer. In return he promised that he would do the first thing that I required of him. Do you deny that, Sir Knight?'

'No,' said the Knight. 'That was our bargain.'

'Then hear my request. Before this court I ask you now to marry me.'

The Knight gasped.

'As I saved your life, it's no more than I deserve.'

'For the love of God, make some other choice. Take all I have, but let my body go.'

'Damn me if I will, and damn you too,' she said. 'I may be old and poor and ugly, but I wouldn't exchange your love for all the gold that's buried in the earth.'

'My love, you call it? You'd drag me down to hell. How could a man in my position make so vile a match?'

But arguing was a waste of breath. There was nothing he could do about it. And they were married the very next morning.

I won't describe for you the joy and splendour of their wedding feast. I expect you think it's because I'm too lazy. In fact, there was neither joy nor splendour, nothing but misery and gloom. He married the old woman in secret, then for the rest of the day hid himself away like an owl. He couldn't bear the sight of her.

That night, in their curtained marriage bed he tossed and turned in agony, while she lay beside him, her face all smiles.

'Bless you, dear husband,' she said. 'Does every knight treat his wife like this? Is it the custom in King Arthur's court? Are all his knights so hard to please? I am your own beloved wife. I saved your life and have never done you any harm. Why do you treat me like this on our wedding night? You behave like a lunatic. What have I done wrong? For the love of God, tell me. If I have any fault, I'll try to mend it if I can.'

'Mend it?' exclaimed the Knight. 'Impossible! You're

so ugly, so old, so poor, so commonly born – these things can't be mended. No wonder I toss and turn. I wish to God my heart would burst.'

'So that's why you're so upset. Well, sir, I daresay I could mend all this in a day or two, if you'd only treat me with a little more respect. Just now you were talking about birth and breeding – the kind that's based on the wealth of ancestors – and you claim that that is what makes you a gentleman. Arrogant rubbish! I wouldn't give a hen for it. The true gentleman is one who lives a blameless life, in public and in private, a man of noble actions. Christ wants us to claim that our nobility comes from him, not from the wealth of ancestors. They can bequeath their wealth to us, but not the noble way of life that makes them gentlemen and which they asked us to follow as best we could. If true nobility could be inherited, then succeeding generations would be paragons of virtue. Yet we're always hearing how outrageously some lord's son is behaving. He may be a duke or an earl, but I still say he's no gentleman, only a lout. True nobility comes from God alone; it cannot be inherited. And so, dear husband, though my ancestors may have been common people, I hope that God Almighty will give me nobility of mind and the grace to live a noble life.

'You reproach me with my poverty. But God himself chose to live in poverty. It's a good thing to be content with little. You reproach me for being old – but men of standing like yourself say that old age should be respected. You reproach me for my ugliness. But doesn't that mean that no one else will fall in love with me and that you'll have me all to yourself?

'Now, sir, I shall give you two choices. Either you can have me old and ugly, but faithful to you till I die, or you can have me young and beautiful and take your chance. Which shall it be?'

The Knight thought hard, but he couldn't make up his mind. At last he said, 'My lady, my love, my dearest wife, I leave the choice to you. Choose whichever's best for both of us. What pleases you will please me too.'

'Am I your master? Can I rule as I wish and have my own way?'

'Yes, wife. I think that's best.'

'Then give me a kiss and don't be angry any more,' she said. 'I shall be both to you – I mean both beautiful and good. If I'm not as good and true a wife to you as ever there was since the world began, may I die in a madhouse. You will find me as beautiful as any lady, queen or empress from east to west. Draw the curtains and look.'

When the Knight saw that it was really so, that she was both young and beautiful, he caught her up in his arms for joy, his heart bathed in happiness. A thousand times he kissed her, and she obeyed him in every way that could content or please him. And they lived in perfect joy to the end of their lives.

That's the end of my tale. May Jesus Christ send us young, submissive husbands, who are good lovers, and the luck to outlive them. May those who won't be ruled by their wives come to an early end. As for cantankerous old skinflints, they can go to the devil.

The Parson

THERE was a Parson, a parish priest in fact,
A poor man, rich in holy thought and act,
A learned scholar, faithful in his preaching
And, with his parish folk, devout in teaching.
He was an active worker, generous, kind,
And patient in adversity, you'd find.
He loathed to excommunicate and curse
Those who paid no tithes, but from his purse
Freely he gave the poor his wherewithal;
He lived on little, and his needs were small.
Though wide his parish, the houses far asunder,
Sickness nor misfortune, rain nor thunder
Stopped his patient visits, staff in hand,
To the lowest born or highest in the land.
He led the way and practised what he taught –
A precept from the Gospel he had caught,
To which he had attached this proverb too:
'If gold can rust, then what will iron do?'

For if a priest be rotten, in whom we trust,
No wonder that a common man can rust.
Let priests be warned: no shepherd should be seen
Covered with dirt and dung, while his sheep go clean.
Instead a priest should always guidance give
By spotless conduct how his flock should live.
He did not put his living out to hire
And leave his sheep to wallow in the mire,
While he ran off to London to St Paul's
And chanted masses for departed souls,
Or earned a lazy living with some guild;
He stayed at home, attending to his fold.
Virtuous, saintly to the manner born,
He never treated sinful men with scorn.
His speech was neither lofty nor severe,
But kind and tactful; his purpose was to steer
His flock to heaven by good example; yet,
If a man – whatever his rank – were obstinate,
His rebuke was sharp and had a stinging sound.
A better priest was nowhere to be found.
The Word of Christ and his apostles twelve
He taught, but first he followed it himself.

The Ploughman

A PLOUGHMAN too, his brother, beside him rode;
He'd carted dung in many a lumbering load.
A good and faithful labourer was he,
Living in peace and perfect charity.
God he loved best, with all his heart and mind,
His neighbour next; he loved all humankind
And would thresh and dig and ditch for Jesus' sake
To help the poor, and yet no payment take.
His settlement of tithes was full and fair;
He rode in a labourer's smock on a humble mare.

The Miller

THERE was a Miller, a man of powerful size;
In wrestling bouts he always won the prize.
Thick-set and muscular, big-boned and raw,
He could heave off from its hinges any door
Or break it down by charging with his head.
His beard, like fox or farmyard sow, was red
And broad as well, shaped like a garden spade.
On the right side of his nose the man displayed
A wart, and on it grew a tuft of hair
Red as the bristles in an old pig's ear.
His nostrils, I could see, were black and wide;
He wore a sword and buckler at his side.
His mouth was vast, wide as a furnace door;
With bawdy tales he liked to hold the floor.

The Miller

Corn he stole and charged three times his due;
But honest millers, I fear, are extremely few.
His coat was white, and blue his hooded crown;
His bagpipe music brought us out of town.

The Steward

THERE was a Steward from the Inns of Court,
A lawyers' housekeeper, the shrewdest sort.
When buying food, whether in cash he paid
Or bought on credit, his purchases were made
With perfect timing – which shows, by God's good grace
The wit of a simple man can quite outpace
The wisdom of a host of learned men.
Of masters had he more than three times ten,
All expert and accomplished in the law,
A dozen of whom were capable, I'm sure,
Of managing estates for any peer
And keeping him out of debt and in the clear,
With sound advice whatever might befall;
And yet this crafty steward could fool them all.

The White Crow

THE STEWARD'S TALE

WHEN Phoebus lived down here on earth, he was (as the old books tell us) the liveliest young knight in the world, and the best archer too. He slew the serpent Python as he lay sleeping in the sun. That was only one of his many splendid deeds. He could also play any instrument and sing the loveliest melodies. Amphion, King of Thebes, whose singing raised the city wall, could not match him as a singer. Phoebus was a man of great distinction, the noblest, most handsome and honourable man since the world began.

Phoebus had in his house a crow which he kept in a cage and taught to speak. It was as white as a snow-white swan and could imitate anybody's speech. No nightingale in the world could sing a hundred thousandth part as sweetly.

Now Phoebus had a wife whom he loved more than life and did his best to please. But he was very jealous and kept a close watch on her. He didn't want to risk being made to look a fool. We all feel like that – but what's the use? There's nothing you can do about it. When you have a good wife, it's a mistake to try to keep an eye on her all the time. A strong instinct is not to be thwarted.

Take a bird, for example. Put it in a cage, and do your best to foster it tenderly with food and drink and every dainty you can think of. Though its cage is of the brightest gold, yet it would twenty thousand times rather live in the cold wild forest and eat worms. All it wants is liberty, and it will always try to escape if it can. Or take a cat. You may feed it with milk and juicy meat and give it a bed of silk. But once it sees a mouse run by the wall, it forgets all that. All it can think of is eating the mouse. Instinct wins.

So it was that Phoebus, who had no guile in him, was in spite of all his fine qualities deceived. His wife became infatuated with another man, who was quite worthless compared with him. And this kind of situation always causes trouble. Once, when Phoebus was out of the house, his wife sent for her fancy man – if you'll forgive the expression. The white crow in its cage saw them together and said never a word. But when Phoebus came home, the crow sang, 'Cuckoo! Cuckoo! Cuckoo!'

'Why, bird!' said Phoebus. 'Whatever's that song you're singing? I've always enjoyed your songs, but this one is different.'

'But it suits the occasion,' said the crow. 'Phoebus, in spite of all your distinction, your grace and musicianship, your wife is deceiving you. You've been hoodwinked by a nobody, a man no better than a gnat compared with you.' And sadly the crow told him what it had seen while he was away, and how shamelessly his wife had behaved.

Phoebus turned his head away, he thought his sorrowful heart would break in two. In his rage he bent his bow, put an arrow to the string, and killed his wife – yes, killed her. Then, suddenly horrified at what he had done, he broke his harp and lute, guitar and psaltery, as well as his bow and arrows, and cried out to the crow, 'Traitor with a scorpion tongue, you have destroyed me. I wish I were dead. My dear wife, you were so faithful and true to me. Now you lie dead, so pale of face, and innocent too – I swear you were innocent. Oh, I was too hasty – I was mad to kill you! We should beware of hastiness and believe nothing without a witness. Oh, I could kill myself for grief!' He looked at the crow and said angrily, 'I'll punish you for this! There was once a time when you could sing like the nightingale; but now you shall lose your song and all your white feathers too. Traitor! You and your offspring will be black for ever. Never in all your life shall you speak again or make sweet music. For ever after, when storm and rain are on the way, you will croak, because it was your fault that my wife was killed.'

He sprang at the crow and pulled out all its white feathers. Then he made it black and took away its song and flung it out of doors as a present to the devil. And that's why all crows are now black.

Gentlemen, don't forget what I've told you. Never tell a man a tale you've heard against his wife, or you will earn his mortal hatred. Whether or not there's any truth in the tale, keep your mouth shut. Remember the crow.

The Bailiff

THE Bailiff was quick to anger, tall and thin;
His beard was closely shaven to the chin,
His hair trimmed in a short and even crop
About the ears, while the head on top
Was shorn like a priest's in front. His legs were lean
And long as sticks; no calf was to be seen.
He supervised both granary and bin;
No auditor could get the better of him.
By noting down the drought and fall of rain,
He knew the yield he'd get from seed and grain.
His master's pigs and poultry, cattle stock,
His horses, dairy, every herd and flock
Were in the Bailiff's own controlling hand.
He'd kept accounts and shown them on demand
Ever since his master's earliest years;
No one had ever caught him in arrears.
Every serf and cowherd on the farm
Feared him like the plague – and did no harm,

For he knew their every trick and every dodge.
Set in a pleasant field, his house or lodge
Was shaded from the sun by leafy trees.
By subtle means he took good care to please
His lord with loans or presents from his goods,
And earned his thanks as well as coats and hoods.
In bargaining he always came off best,
And showed great skill in feathering his nest.
He was a Norfolk man, as I heard tell,
And came from a village close to Baldeswell;
In youth he'd been a carpenter by trade.
Dressed in blue, he carried a rusty blade
And rode, last in line, at a gentle trot
A sturdy dapple-grey whose name was Scot.

The Summoner

THERE was a Summoner with us in that place,
Who had a fiery-red cherubic face.
His black and scabby brows, his scraggy beard
And pimpled cheeks were a sight that children feared.
There was no mercury with powerful bite
Nor white lead ointment that could cure the blight
Of boils and pimples sitting on his cheeks.
Garlic he loved, and onions too and leeks,
And drinking draughts of strongest wine, blood-red.
Then he would shout, like one whose wits had fled,
And when he was drunk begin to jabber and bray
In Latin – he heard the language every day
And knew some tags and phrases, two or three
That parrot-wise he'd learnt from some decree.

If tested, he ran out of learned chatter
And cried, 'What does the law say on this matter?'
He was an easy-going chap and kind,
As nice a fellow as you could hope to find;
Yet he could cheat an innocent on the sly.
He kept the parish youth under his eye
And counselled them; they listened to what he said.
He wore a garland of flowers on his head,
Like one outside a tavern hung on a stake.
He played the fool with a shield – it was made of cake.

The Pardoner

THERE rode with him (I bring my list to an end)
A Pardoner from Charing Cross, his friend.
He'd come from the court of Rome quite recently
And boldly chanted, 'Come, my love, to me,'
While louder than the loudest trumpet rang
The bass accompaniment the Summoner sang.
This Pardoner had hair as yellow as wax
Hanging smoothly like a hank of flax,
In wispy strands over his shoulders spread.
For fun he wore no hood upon his head;
Inside his bag he kept it, safely stowed.
In the latest style, it seemed to him, he rode;
Save for a little cap, his head was bare,
And he had staring eye-balls, like a hare.
He'd sewn a holy relic on his cap.
In front of him his bag lay in his lap,
Brought from Rome, with pardons stuffed to the brim.
His voice, a goat-like bleat, was small and thin;
He had no beard, and none was coming on –
Not a hair was on his chin, or sign of one;
He reminded me of a gelding or a mare.
As for his trade, from Berwick down to Ware
There was no Pardoner could take his place.
Inside his bag he kept a pillow-case,
And this he vowed to be Our Lady's veil.
He claimed he had a snippet of the sail
Of St Peter's boat, when rashly far from land
He walked the waves, till saved by Jesus' hand.
He had a metal cross inlaid with stones
And in a vessel of glass a pig's bones,
With which he made more money in one day

Than a country priest in months could put away.
So, by hollow flattery and deceit
He managed priest and people both to cheat.
But to give the man his due, first and last
In church he was a fine ecclesiast.
How well he read a lesson and told a story!
But best of all he sang the offertory,
Knowing full well that when his song was sung
He had to preach and polish smooth his tongue
To wheedle silver coins from the crowd;
Therefore he sang both merrily and loud.

In Search of Death

THE PARDONER'S TALE

In Flanders there was once a company of young people who spent their time in every kind of folly, rioting, gambling, dancing and dicing day and night, eating and drinking to excess, and swearing grisly oaths.

Early one morning, three of these gamblers, who had sat up drinking at an inn all night, heard the clink of a bell outside. It was ringing a coffin to the grave.

'Whose corpse is this?' said one of them. And he called to his boy to go and find out.

'No need, sir,' said the boy. 'I was told who it was two hours before you came here. It was an old friend of yours. He died suddenly during the night. He was sitting upright on his bench, very drunk, when along came a sneaking thief called Death and drove a spear through his heart. He's killing everybody in the district. It's the plague – there have been a thousand deaths already. We may all have to face him, so my mother tells me. And that goes for you too, sir. You'd better look out.'

'Holy Mary!' cried the innkeeper. 'The boy's quite

right. A mile away from here, in the village, Death has this year killed off man, woman, child, labourer and page – everyone. I think he must live there. So be careful!'

'What!' said the gambler. 'Is Death so dangerous to meet? By God's sacred bones, I'll go after him. I'll search for him in the streets. Listen, lads, we three are one. Let's swear everlasting brotherhood, and we'll kill this false traitor Death.'

The three of them swore solemnly to live and die for one another, as though they were true brothers. And they lurched off towards the village the innkeeper had spoken of, swearing with many a grisly oath that Death should die.

They had not gone half a mile when, just as they were about to cross a stile, they met a very old man.

'God bless you, gentlemen!' said the old man courteously.

'Get out of the way, you fool,' said the most arrogant of the three gamblers. 'Why are you so muffled up? And how have you managed to live so ridiculously long?'

The old man looked him straight in the face. 'Sir,' he said, 'even if I were to walk as far as India, I would never in town or village find anyone willing to exchange his youth for my years. So I must keep my age for as long as God requires. Not even Death will take my life. So I walk about like a restless prisoner all day long, knocking with my stick on the earth, my mother's door, saying, "Dear mother, let me in. See how I'm shrivelling up, flesh and blood and skin. Oh, when will my bones be at rest? Mother, I would gladly exchange all my wardrobe of clothes for a winding sheet to wrap me in my coffin." But she will not listen, and that's why my face is so pale and shrunken. But, sirs, you should not speak so insultingly to an old man who has done you no harm. You may live to be as old yourselves. God bless you, wherever you go. I must go too – I have business to do.'

'Not yet, you old fool,' said the gambler. 'Stay where

you are. You spoke just now of that traitor Death who's killing off all our friends. I believe you're his spy. You're in league with him to kill us young people. Tell me where he is or, by God, you shall pay for it!'

'Well, sirs, if you're so keen to find Death, turn up this twisting path. I left him up there under a tree, and he'll be there still. He won't run away, for all your ranting. Do you see that oak? You'll find him there. And may God, who saved mankind, save you too!'

The three gamblers ran to the tree, and there they found not a man but a pile of fine gold florins, about seven bushels. They were so delighted with the gold that they gave up their search for Death and sat down beside the precious hoard. The worst of the three was the first to speak.

'Listen, brothers,' he said, 'I've got sense in my head, though I do like to fool around. Fortune has given us this treasure to enjoy for the rest of our lives. Who would have thought that we'd have such good luck? All this gold is ours, of course. If it could be taken home to my house – or to yours, if you like – that would be fine. But obviously that can't be done in the daytime. People would say we were thieves and have us hanged for stealing our own treasure. It must be done by night. I suggest that we draw lots. Whoever draws the shortest straw shall run to the town and bring us bread and wine, while the other two stay and guard the treasure. When night comes, we'll take it to whatever place we decide on.'

So they drew lots. And the shortest straw fell to the youngest, who at once set off for the town.

As soon as he'd gone, one gambler said to the other, 'You're my sworn brother, as you know. Our friend has gone, and here's all this gold to be divided between the three of us. But if I could fix things so that it could be shared between us two, wouldn't I be doing you a good turn?'

'You'd never get away with it. He knows that the gold is here with us. What shall we say to him? What shall we do?'

'I'll tell you. We are two, and two are stronger than one. Well, when he's sitting down, get up as if you wanted to have a bit of sport with him. While you're pretending to wrestle, I'll plunge my dagger into his side, and so must you. Then, my dear friend, all this gold can be divided between the two of us. And we can gamble away to our hearts' content.'

So they agreed to kill him.

Meanwhile the youngest gambler, who was on his way to the town, kept rolling up and down in his heart the beauty of those bright new florins. 'Oh Lord,' he said, 'if only I could have all this treasure for myself alone, no man under the sun would live as happily as I.'

In the end our enemy, the devil, gave him the idea of buying poison to kill his two friends. So he found a chemist in the town and asked him for some poison. He said it was to get rid of his rats – also a polecat that was after his chickens.

'I'll give you some,' said the chemist, 'which is so strong that it will kill any creature that eats no more than a grain. Before you have time to walk a mile, it will be dead.'

The wretch took the box of poison in his hand and ran into the next street. Here he borrowed three bottles. Into two of them he poured the poison, but the third he kept clean for his own use, for he intended to spend the night carrying off the gold. Then he filled his three bottles with wine and returned to his friends.

Well, there's no need to make a long story of it. His two friends killed him right away, as they had planned.

'Now let's sit down and drink and enjoy ourselves,' said the one to the other. 'We'll bury his body later.'

He picked up a bottle – it happened to be one with poison in – and drank from it and passed it on to the other. And so they both died.

The Poet, Geoffrey Chaucer, Says Good-bye

IF there is anything in this book that you have enjoyed, then give thanks to God, the source of all wisdom and excellence. If there is anything you dislike, then put it down to my incompetence. I would have done better if I could.

MORE ABOUT THE PILGRIMS AND THEIR TALES

17 *palmers*: originally, pilgrims to the Holy Land; later, pilgrims generally.

18 *the Tabard Inn in Southwark*: Southwark is the district south of London Bridge and outside the city wall. It had a number of inns, and travellers who wanted to avoid the crush of traffic when the Bridge gate opened at sunrise stayed here overnight. The Tabard Inn was there in Chaucer's day and was burnt down in 1676. A tabard was a short sleeveless coat, embroidered with armorial bearings, such as a herald wore.

Our Host was Harry Bailey, a real person. Besides being an innkeeper, he was twice a burgess (similar to an M.P.) for the borough. Chaucer is almost sure to have known him, and he may even have made the pilgrimage to Canterbury with him.

marshal in a hall: master of ceremonies.

19 *St Thomas's watering-place*: a brook by the Old Kent Road, about half an hour's ride from Southwark. The Pilgrims' Way went through Deptford, Blackheath, Dartford, Rochester, Sittingbourne and Ospringe.

20 *The Knight* was an aristocrat. His chivalric ideals were already old-fashioned by Chaucer's day, and the poet idealizes him. The campaigns he took part in – against the Moors, the Turks and the Slavs – were real ones. It was quite usual for knights to serve in foreign countries that were at war, especially in the cause of Christendom.

22 PRISONERS OF WAR: This heroic and romantic tale is one which would obviously have appealed to the Knight. Chaucer adapted it freely from the Italian poet Boccaccio.

29 *lists*: palisades enclosing the tilting-ground.

35 *fury*: an avenging or tormenting spirit.

41 *a mighty bow*: the long bow, like Robin Hood's bow. The Yeoman, the Knight's servant and forester, was an expert archer. The long bow came originally from Wales and was adopted in the fourteenth century as the English national weapon. It could pierce armour and had a greater range and accuracy than the cross-bow, which it replaced.

St Christopher was the patron saint of foresters and travellers.

42 *The Prioress* was the senior nun in charge of a convent. In addition to her religious duties, she also took in as boarders the daughters of well-to-do families. She taught them manners, deportment, and perhaps a little reading. Grammar schools were for boys only. The Prioress was also known as Madam Eglantine – or Lady Sweetbriar. Chaucer writes wittily about the way she spoke French, about her worldly tastes and dainty table manners. In those days fingers were often used rather than knives and forks, and bones and scraps were thrown onto the rush-strewn floor for the dogs.

43 *wimple*: a linen covering for the head and neck, worn by nuns.

44 *The Nun's Priest*: Chaucer does not say much about him in the Prologue. These lines come later on, in the Prologue to the Nun's Priest's Tale, which is one of the best. It is narrated by the priest accompanying the Prioress.

45 THE COCK AND THE FOX: An animal fable to illustrate the lesson 'beware of flattery'. A story with a moral would of course appeal to the priest.

there was no chimney – only a hole in the roof above the open hearth, to let out the smoke. A simple house like the widow's was probably built of timber and plaster and had two storeys, with a kitchen living room and one bedroom for the whole household. It must have been very draughty. Windows, usually without glass, had wooden shutters which were closed at night.

48 *Mulier est hominis confusio* means exactly the opposite of

Chanticleer's translation. It really means 'woman is a confounded nuisance to man'.

51 *Jack Straw and his mob*: This refers to the Peasants' Revolt of 1381, when Jack Straw led an attack on London from Blackheath. There was a massacre of Flemish wool-traders, whose competition the peasants resented. As he was living at Aldgate, Chaucer must have seen and heard something of the disturbances. This is one of the few occasions when he refers to contemporary events.

53 *The Monk* belonged to the Benedictine Order and had taken the three vows of poverty, chastity and obedience. But he had little interest in religion. Extremely worldly, he loved riding, hunting and rich food; he wore squirrel fur, which was not allowed.

55 *The Friar*, another corrupt member of the church, was supposed to set an example of Christian living. Instead of helping the sick and the poor as he should, he preferred the company of innkeepers and barmaids.

57 *The Merchant* was probably a wool merchant. One of his main concerns was to keep the stretch of sea between Ipswich and Middelburg free from pirates. These ports handled the export of wool.

58 *The Scholar*, an Oxford University student training for a master's degree, was eager to learn and sincere in his religious beliefs. In England, Oxford and Cambridge were the only universities. There were few textbooks, and students learnt mainly by taking down a lecturer's words and memorizing them. With no spare money for clothes or good food, the Scholar refused to take a lay job, even though he had as yet no income from the church.

60 PATIENT GRISELDA is based on a story by the Italian poet, Petrarch. Though to us today Griselda's blind obedience to her husband may seem extreme, if not ridiculous, in Chaucer's day the story was popular, especially with men. But it would hardly have appealed to the Wife of Bath, who believes, as her story shows, that the wife should be the boss. The Scholar does not suggest that all women should follow

Griselda's example. He is concerned to show the virtue of patient endurance in adversity.

72 *The Poet, Geoffrey Chaucer*: These words of the Host to Chaucer come later in the poem, before the poet begins his Tale of Sir Topaz. They are included here because they describe the poet's appearance and manner.

73 *The Sea Captain* was a capable seaman whose trading ship sailed between Bordeaux and Dartmouth. The source of his story A HUNDRED-FRANC LOAN is not known.

80 *The five guildsmen* were wealthy enough to bring their own cook with them. Perhaps they were nervous about the sort of food wayside inns would provide. Like the wool trade, most industries were run by master craftsmen, and each had its own guild – the Carpenters' Guild, the Weavers' Guild, and so on. These were the forerunners of the modern trade unions. They gave their members certain privileges, they fixed wages, laid down working conditions and saw that honest prices were charged and sound materials used. They also helped widows and orphans as well as the sick.

81 *The Cook* owned a fly-infested food shop in London, where (said the Host later) he sold stale parsley and twice warmed-up pies. He also hired himself out privately to rich clients as a professional cook.

81 *galingale*: spiced root.

82 *The Judge* was a barrister and learned lawyer of the front rank. There were about twenty of them altogether, and the judges of the King's court were chosen from their number.

83 THE WILD WAVES is, like the story of Griselda, a folk tale about wronged wives. It praises Christian virtues, especially constancy. In giving this tale to the Judge, perhaps Chaucer is indirectly suggesting that these are the kind of qualities you would expect to find in so eminent a man.

95 *The Franklin* was a wealthy and influential landowner who had served as a Knight of the Shire and held several Crown appointments. He was very hospitable and enjoyed rich food.

to serve the sauce unspiced: For flavouring meat (in winter and spring only salt meat was available) the cook depended on a variety of spiced sauces. The fishpond, a luxury that few could afford, ensured a supply of fresh fish. Vegetables were less plentiful than they are today. There were peas, beans, cabbages and onions, but no potatoes and no swedes.

97 THE BLACK ROCKS OF BRITTANY is based on an old folk tale common to many languages, about a lady who promises herself to a man on condition that he performs a task which she believes to be impossible. This graceful romantic story, in which the black rocks symbolize the misfortunes and disasters of life, admirably suits the wise and genial Franklin.

107 *The Doctor* was shrewd and thrifty. Chaucer praises him for his skill in diagnosis, as well as for his thorough knowledge of medical textbooks. Illness was treated at home, not in hospital. Most people relied on some homely remedy provided by family or friends, and only the rich could afford a doctor. His recommended fee was five pounds – more than a year's wages for many people then – and it was common practice to demand the fee before treatment was started. This consisted mainly of bleeding or purging. The medicine prescribed had an astrological basis and could only be given at the right time – when planetary influences favoured the patient. Magic charms were also thought to help with the cure.

108 *The Wife of Bath*: This bouncing, five times married and much travelled housewife, aggressive, vulgar, addicted to huge hats and startling colours, is a splendid creation. As for the tale she tells, about an old hag's transformation into a beautiful young girl, could it be that the Wife of Bath wished she could herself reverse the ageing process and recapture all the delights of her youth?

116 *The Parson* is Chaucer's portrait of the ideal parish priest. He is the only churchman he finds wholly to be admired. In those days it was all too common for a priest to abandon his parish for easier money. Jobs such as singing masses for the dead or acting as chaplain to a guild were less exacting

and much better paid. In this Parson Chaucer rejoiced to find a man of integrity.

122 THE WHITE CROW is based on an ancient folk fable about a talking bird punished for revealing intimate secrets in its chatter. Chaucer's version comes from the Latin poet Ovid. Phoebus Apollo, traditionally the Greek god of music and poetry and of high moral principles, is shown in *The White Crow* as a pampered nobleman, jealous, over-hasty, self-deluding and vindictive. At first he believes the crow's story of his wife's infidelity and kills her. Next moment he persuades himself that she was innocent and that the crow had lied. One of several morals in this brief tale is that over-hasty reaction can all too easily result in disaster.

127 *The Summoner* was an officer who served a court summons on offenders against church laws.

128 *cake* is a large, flat, unleavened biscuit. The Summoner was clowning, and holding it as if it were a shield.

129 *The Pardoner* was a clergyman authorized by the Pope to sell pardons. If sinners bought these they were excused part of the penance imposed, so this practice was regarded as a short cut to God's forgiveness. There were plenty of fraudulent pardoners about. As Chaucer's Pardoner was drunk and on holiday with strangers he would not meet again, he did not mind admitting his dishonesty.

131 IN SEARCH OF DEATH: Set against the background of the Black Death, this is perhaps the most dramatic of the tales.

It's the plague: The Black Death is the modern name for a deadly form of bubonic plague which was carried across Europe by black rats in the fourteenth century. In 1348–9 it wiped out a third or possibly even half of the population of England. Dirt and lack of sanitation helped to spread it, and the towns and ports were the worst affected. Agriculture was badly hit; economic, religious and artistic life was seriously disrupted. Medical knowledge was quite unable to control it. Outbreaks occurred at intervals till late in the seventeenth century, when the black rat was expelled by the brown, which did not carry the infection.

ALSO IN

HEINEMANN NEW WINDMILLS

Founding Editors: Anne and Ian Serraillier

Chinua Achebe Things Fall Apart
Douglas Adams The Hitchhiker's Guide to the Galaxy
Vivien Alcock The Cuckoo Sister; The Monster Garden; The Trial of Anna Cotman; A Kind of Thief
Margaret Atwood The Handmaid's Tale
J G Ballard Empire of the Sun
Nina Bawden The Witch's Daughter; A Handful of Thieves; Carrie's War; The Robbers; Devil by the Sea; Kept in the Dark; The Finding; Keeping Henry; Humbug
E R Braithwaite To Sir, With Love
John Branfield The Day I Shot My Dad
F Hodgson Burnett The Secret Garden
Ray Bradbury The Golden Apples of the Sun; The Illustrated Man
Betsy Byars The Midnight Fox; Goodbye, Chicken Little; The Pinballs
Victor Canning The Runaways; Flight of the Grey Goose
Ann Coburn Welcome to the Real World
Hannah Cole Bring in the Spring
Jane Leslie Conly Racso and the Rats of NIMH
Robert Cormier We All Fall Down
Roald Dahl Danny, The Champion of the World; The Wonderful Story of Henry Sugar; George's Marvellous Medicine; The BFG; The Witches; Boy; Going Solo; Charlie and the Chocolate Factory; Matilda
Anita Desai The Village by the Sea
Charles Dickens A Christmas Carol; Great Expectations
Peter Dickinson The Gift; Annerton Pit; Healer
Berlie Doherty Granny was a Buffer Girl
Gerald Durrell My Family and Other Animals
J M Falkner Moonfleet
Anne Fine The Granny Project
Anne Frank The Diary of Anne Frank
Leon Garfield Six Apprentices
Jamila Gavin The Wheel of Surya
Adele Geras Snapshots of Paradise

Graham Greene The Third Man and The Fallen Idol; Brighton Rock

Thomas Hardy The Withered Arm and Other Wessex Tales

Rosemary Harris Zed

L P Hartley The Go-Between

Ernest Hemingway The Old Man and the Sea; A Farewell to Arms

Nat Hentoff Does this School have Capital Punishment?

Nigel Hinton Getting Free; Buddy; Buddy's Song

Minfong Ho Rice Without Rain

Anne Holm I Am David

Janni Howker Badger on the Barge; Isaac Campion

Linda Hoy Your Friend Rebecca

Barbara Ireson (Editor) In a Class of Their Own

Jennifer Johnston Shadows on Our Skin

Toeckey Jones Go Well, Stay Well

James Joyce A Portrait of the Artist as a Young Man

Geraldine Kaye Comfort Herself; A Breath of Fresh Air

Clive King Me and My Million

Dick King-Smith The Sheep-Pig

Daniel Keyes Flowers for Algernon

Elizabeth Laird Red Sky in the Morning; Kiss the Dust

D H Lawrence The Fox and The Virgin and the Gypsy; Selected Tales

Harper Lee To Kill a Mockingbird

Julius Lester Basketball Game

Ursula Le Guin A Wizard of Earthsea

C Day Lewis The Otterbury Incident

David Line Run for Your Life; Screaming High

Joan Lingard Across the Barricades; Into Exile; The Clearance; The File on Fraulein Berg

Penelope Lively The Ghost of Thomas Kempe

Jack London The Call of the Wild; White Fang

Bernard Mac Laverty Cal; The Best of Bernard Mac Laverty

Margaret Mahy The Haunting; The Catalogue of The Universe

Jan Mark Do You Read Me? Eight Short Stories

James Vance Marshall Walkabout

Somerset Maugham The Kite and Other Stories

Michael Morpurgo Waiting for Anya; My Friend Walter; The War of Jenkins' Ear

How many have you read?